WOODY AND JUNE VERSUS THE END

WOODY AND JUNE VERSUS THE END

WOODY AND JUNE VERSUS THE APOCALYPSE, EPISODE 17

ROBERT J. MCCARTER

LITTLE HUMMINGBIRD PUBLISHING

Woody and June versus the End

Woody and June versus the Apocalypse, Episode 17

Cover photography courtesy the Grand Canyon National Park

"Zombies Ahead" image by ducu59us

Version 1.0, May 2024

ISBN: 978-1-963354-07-2

Find out more about this book at: WoodyAndJune.com

Visit Robert's website at: RobertJMcCarter.com

Published by:

Little Hummingbird Publishing

P.O. Box 23518

Flagstaff, AZ 86002

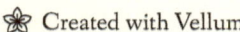 Created with Vellum

WOODY AND JUNE VERSUS THE APOCALYPSE

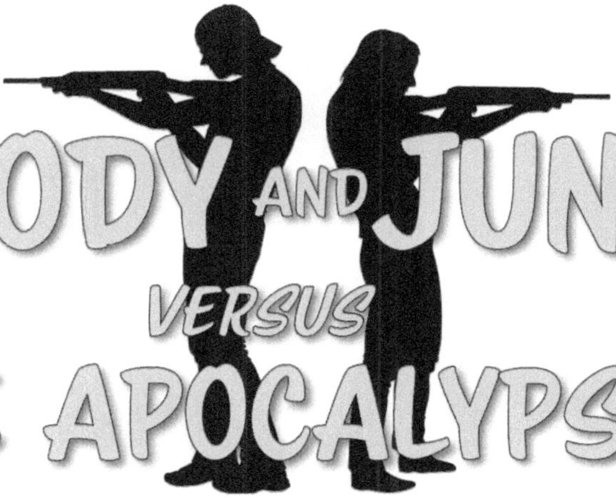

WOODY AND JUNE VERSUS THE APOCALYPSE

There are currently 17 episodes of *Woody and June versus the Apocalypse,* but episodes are collected into novel-length volumes with a larger story arc. This is the most economical way to consume these stories:

- Woody and June Versus the Apocalypse: Volume 1 (Episodes 1 - 7)
- Woody and June Versus the Apocalypse: Volume 2 (Episodes 8 - 12)
- Woody and June Versus the Apocalypse: Volume 3 (Episodes 13 - 17)

To stay abreast of all things Woody and June, head over to *Woody AndJune.com* and sign up for my e-mail newsletter so you don't miss out on a thing! Plus, you'll get a free ebook that includes "Park's Law of the Apocalypse," a newsletter-exclusive story in the world of Woody and June.

CHAPTER ONE

JUNE HAS me hopped up on steroids.

I love it and I hate it.

I love that I feel a lot more like myself, that the growing loudness of the zombie group mind has faded, that I can tap into it when I need to but it doesn't feel like I am drowning in it anymore. I love that I have the energy to stand, even enough energy to pace.

"Are you okay?" June asks with a small smile. June Medina is in her element, a petite goddess of war with a round face, olive skin, short black hair, and ocean-blue eyes. She seems to be lit up by the challenge that faces us because we are going to war.

I've been pacing over the worn wooden floor of the dining hall of Phantom Ranch not far from the Colorado River at the bottom of the Grand Canyon. The tables have been shoved to the side, and June, my best friend Dallas, and several other survivors have been gathered around it while I pace.

I nod and say, "Steroids."

Because of her short stature and pixie-cut hair, June looks like the kind of woman who, before it all went to shit, would get cast as an elf around Christmas. But looks are deceiving. She's ex-army and as tough as they come, really better built for this time than I am.

"Save some of that energy," she says. "And don't forget to gather that intel."

I nod and look down at the "smart" phone in my hand. I put smart in quotes because without the internet it's not so smart. But I always have a couple because GPS still works and some of these have music on them and books.

Any music in an apocalypse. Seriously. I used to be pretty judgmental of certain genres—looking at you folk, jazz, and country—but the potluck nature of these phones has widened my tastes considerably.

June smiles and walks back to the table and the discussion there, all straight backed and confident.

She's been asking me if I'm okay a lot in the past few hours. After what Dallas and I have just been through, it's understandable. Hell, after what we've all been through in the last six weeks, that question is universally applicable.

Today is day thirty-nine of Woody and June versus the Apocalypse. That small number absolutely can't possibly contain the magnitude of what we have experienced since June and I met at a dog food plant in Flagstaff, Arizona.

We've been all over Northern Arizona, in and out of the Grand Canyon fighting zombies and psychotic, petty, wannabe warlords. We fell in love, kind of broke up, and got back together, sort of. We met Dallas along the way and the three of us have become a team, each one of us being captured in turn, sometimes more than once, having to be rescued by the others.

You see, the worst psychotic, petty, wannabe warlord, Talia, is June's ex, and Talia has been playing a sick game with us to slowly extract her revenge on June for rejecting her. Twice. The first time when June faked her death via zombie in Albuquerque and the second time when she chose me over Talia here at Phantom Ranch.

The psychotic and the petty don't take well to rejection. Talia is just one of those people that seemed to be waiting for the apocalypse to happen. And she's trying to erase the "wannabe" from the term I use for people like her. She is expanding her territory and is on her way to becoming a real warlord. But there is no getting rid of the "psychotic" and "petty" when it comes to her.

June and I stumbled on to Talia on day nine and all the days since have been about Talia's game and her revenge. Thirty days of this insanity.

That started to change on day twenty-seven when I received dozens of zombie scratches rescuing Dallas in Winslow, Arizona. Dallas wasn't supposed to survive that day and those scratches should have killed me and turned me into a Z. We both survived, but the fungal infection that drives the zombies, that has transformed the world, is still in me and a part of me.

To be fair, that fungal infection is in all of us. You die, you turn. But something very strange happened from those scratches and now I am part of the zombie group mind.

Dallas slowly walks over, leaning heavily on her gnarled wood cane. She's curvy with shoulder-length brown hair and deep frown lines that turn into amazing laugh lines when she's happy. She's in her early thirties, a few years older than June and me. Her jeans and T-shirt are filthy, but given the last few hours and the suicide vest that Talia forced her to wear, it's a much better look.

The right side of her face is bruised and swollen—yes, Talia again —and her right ankle is swollen too much to even wear a boot—that wasn't caused by Talia, not directly, but aggravated by her—but Dallas is alive and that's pretty much everything these days.

"Thanks for not eating me, Woody," she says, smiling.

"You already thanked me," I say, eyeing her. The latest episode of Talia's game left me and Dallas trussed up together dangling from a rope to try to keep that murder vest from going off.

While we were like that, my fever got worse, and the infection took a greater hold of me. Since I was part of the group mind, I could feel the Zs' hunger and their need, and it took everything I had not to bite into Dallas as we hung there cheek to cheek.

That's the dark side of being a node on the mesh network that is the Zs' group mind. The other side—I can't exactly call it "light"—is that I can tap into their cooperative fresh brains radar and know where the living and the Zs all are. I can even participate in the "discussion" the group mind is having about Phantom Ranch and the survivors down here, but that is a lot harder to do.

That's what June was referring to when she mentioned me gathering "intel." I've proved to the survivors here at Phantom Ranch that I know things I shouldn't, but they don't know about the zombie group mind, but June and Dallas do. I've got on a long-sleeved shirt, despite the late spring heat, and half gloves to cover the raw and ragged zombie scratches which just won't heal and have a thin thread of white running through them.

That's the fungus that my body is fighting now with the aid of all those steroids that have me hopped up.

"I did thank you before," Dallas says with a shrug. "Don't think I'll get over saying it for a while." Her brow furrows and she stares at me. "Are you all right?"

"I'm okay," I say. "It's the steroids. I know we need to plan. To think things through. But I just..." I end up taking a deep breath and clenching my hands.

There's a lot to plan. You see, there are two wars we are getting ready to wage. One with Talia and the troops that are heading down from both the North and South Rims, and one with the newly intelligent zombie pods that have staged themselves around Phantom Ranch and this group of survivors.

Yeah. When I write it this quickly it all seems like a lot. But, as I do with all these diaries, I feel the need to summarize things a bit when I start a new diary since I have no idea how many of these will survive. If any. I have no idea how much longer June, Dallas, and I have, much less the human race.

Hopefully, my other diaries survived and this is not the first of them that you are reading. If it is, just trust me, the zombie apocalypse didn't turn out quite like it did in the comic books and movies.

Although, I must say that they all predicted people like Talia. Human nature, I guess.

The Phantom Ranch dining hall is simple, made of rustic wood with high ceilings and a view of the varied deciduous trees outside, mostly cottonwoods and a few fruit trees here and there. It's late spring, almost summer so the green of the trees is still light and hopeful, but the atmosphere in this room is anything but.

It smells like a dining hall in here with the lingering odor of decades of steak and stew and baked potatoes. I'm unusually well fed for the apocalypse, but the smell combined with the steroids makes me so hungry. Or maybe that's just the zombie group mind.

Dallas eyes me and nods over to the table where June and five other people are. "You trust them?" she asks, her voice low.

There's June, an older guy with a ponytail named Meryl, Wade, Talia's former gadget guy who looks kind of like a classic geek with glasses and a paunchy belly, a young woman with a military background named Lisa, and two big military looking guys named Milo and Ralph.

It's the latter two Dallas is referring to. During the last episode of the "game," the one that found Dallas wearing a suicide vest and the two of us dangling above an old mule corral down here, we were guarded by what I was calling "beefy boys." These were Talia's enforcers, the ones making sure Dallas and I followed the rules of that cruel game of hers. Milo and Ralph are two of those enforcers, but they have changed sides and questioning their loyalties is entirely relevant.

They are both young, strong, and know how to use a gun. Kind of the strong, silent types that are hard to read. Like, really hard to read. Neither of them talk.

Milo was born deaf, and as I glance over, Lisa is signing with him. Ralph lost his tongue to Talia—he said something she didn't like and this was her punishment.

I shrug. "They are more like us than most of the people down here."

Everyone here has experienced Talia's not so gentle leadership style. As June tells it, after things went to shit, Talia was strong and sure of herself and people gathered around her. They followed her here to Phantom Ranch. They had a pretty good thing going, and while Talia wasn't a gentle leader, she kept them all safe.

And then June and I got chased down into the canyon by a zombie tourist horde and Talia found out that June was alive. That she had faked her death. And Talia lost it. She's been messing with us since and getting worse by the day. After Dallas and I rescued June, Talia lost control of Phantom Ranch. But she followed us out, took control over a highly militarized group of survivors in Flagstaff, and then came back and took back over Phantom Ranch.

Writing it all this quickly just sounds insane, I know. But each of those sentences is one or two of these diaries. It's been crazy.

While Dallas and I dangled over that corral, June took Phantom Ranch back over. We haven't had much time to talk, but it doesn't sound like it was that hard. Most of them were over Talia's insanity.

And that was part of Talia's game, part of the endgame that Talia wants to play out. And that is Talia marching here with her much better trained forces from Flagstaff to take Phantom Ranch back by force, extracting her final revenge from June, which, of course, involves a very messy death for Dallas and me.

Dallas is staring at me, her question of trusting Milo and Ralph still hanging in the air. They could be plants. Maybe Talia in her psychotic brilliance planned that far ahead. But these guys know what they are doing, unlike many of the Phantom Ranch survivors, and we need them.

"Wouldn't you jump at the first chance you got if Talia cut your tongue out?" I ask quietly.

Dallas chews on her lip and nods. "We don't know what else she did to them," she whispers.

I nod. "So watch them, Dallas. But I think they're okay. I think they're with us."

She bites her lip and nods. I turn my back to the group, close my eyes, and tap into the zombie group mind. "The intel is in," I say loud enough so they can hear me. "It's time to get Talia on the radio."

CHAPTER TWO

BEFORE I MET JUNE, I was a dedicated go-it-alone survivor. I had been with another group in Phoenix, with another psychotic, petty, wannabe warlord, and that had gone so badly that I had decided to live out the rest of my days alone. I honestly didn't expect there to be very many days.

And then came June and I was sunk.

So when Dallas and I get to the well-worn wooden table in the dining hall of Phantom Ranch and everyone is staring at me, I feel my heart speed up and my mouth goes dry. There are so many ways for things with groups of humans to go south. Hell, the dynamics with just June, Dallas, and myself have gotten complicated lately. And this was a fact before the apocalypse when things were pretty civil, but now that the civilization is gone, it's way more of a high-wire act.

I swallow hard. "Talia and her people on the Bright Angel Trail have just hit Indian Gardens." I wave my phone as if to emphasize that there is some kind of technological explanation for what I know. "I think that's far enough. We need to contact her."

I look at Wade. I've categorized him as a geek because of his black-rimmed glasses and his obvious facility with technology. He's one of the reasons Talia's games got so hard—he has been using a lot of the tech and tricks I have been. But I hadn't really looked at him that closely. Yes, he is short and a bit round around the middle—which is an accomplishment this far into the apocalypse. He also has curly black hair that is getting long enough to cover his forehead and sad grey eyes.

He's about forty and, honestly, looks more like a father to me up close, or a high school teacher. Geeky, yes, and that's a good thing these days, but more than just a geek.

"They've been radioing every fifteen minutes," Wade says, his eyes flicking to the rest of the group. "They don't know Talia has lost control. There have just been no communications since..." He ends up nodding at June.

"What's the play?" Lisa asks. She's a wiry black woman, about five-five, somewhere in her late thirties with extremely short hair and perfect posture. She joined up with Talia and June back in Albuquerque last year and served in Afghanistan like the two of them did.

"I reissue my challenge," I say with a shrug. "The two of us on the bridge. She can bring two people with her as witness but she leaves the rest of her people at Indian Gardens and stops the group coming down from the North Rim. I can bring two people with me. Hand-to-hand combat."

"Why would she do that?" Lisa asks. I don't know Lisa well at all, but there is a frankness and directness to her that I like. June is between Lisa and me, a small smile playing on her lips.

I shrug and say, "She hates me and doesn't think I have a chance of—"

I see a flash of movement, my brain registers that Lisa is moving, and then I'm flat on the wooden floor with my breath knocked out of me.

"And how you gonna win a fight with her?" Lisa asks with a smile, the cold of her knife pressed against my throat.

I would like to say that if I had been in better shape I would have seen it coming and been able to do something about it. But I don't know if that would be honest.

I cough, and when I can breathe again I say, "Unlike you, she will take the time to gloat."

"And then what?" she asks, her knife still pressed to my throat.

"And then I act like a man who has nothing to lose," I say.

Lisa's eyes are a deep, dark brown and she stares unblinkingly at me. "But you are a man with much to lose," she says. She doesn't break eye contact but nods her head towards June and Dallas who are standing above us with amused smiles on their faces. "Why don't you all just get in a raft and go? Why do you care what happens down here?"

Out of my peripheral vision, I can see the smile melt off of June's face. "Talia wasn't awful until we showed up," I say slowly, choosing my words carefully. This is June's burden, June's issue, but June, Dallas, and I are a family and we carry such burdens together. "She's been a wrecking ball since then and we feel some responsibility."

"And..." Lisa prompts, prodding me with her knife.

This has gone on longer than I expected. This isn't a fun little exchange anymore with Lisa proving a valid point. This has turned into a test. I see June's hand straying to the gun on her belt and I sense everyone's hearts kicking into high gear.

June may have wrested control from Talia, may have gotten a couple of the beefy boys to defect, but that doesn't mean we can keep that control.

"*And,*" I begin, spitting the word out and letting some of my anger show. "She shot me in the head. *And* she forced June and me into the Apache Death Caves and reproduced the conditions of that tragic event. *And* she chained Dallas to a statue in Winslow, Arizona, and unleashed the entire zombie population of the town on us. There were thousands of them. *And* she blew up our truck. *And* she chained me to a fence for the Zs to come eat. *And* she left us stranded in a treehouse built in a cell tower with thousands of Zs keeping watch on us."

What I don't say is, "And I'm going to die anyway." Instead I say, "Isn't that enough of a reason? She won't stop chasing us until we are dead or she is dead. I had a shot at her before and blew it. I won't this time."

Lisa's face starts to form a sarcastic smile and the steroid-fueled anger in me just explodes. I don't even think about the knife at my throat and shove her in the chest with the flat of my palms as hard as I can.

I'm not what I would call a beefy boy, but all those years playing baseball left me with a lot of upper body strength. I weigh a lot more than she does and she goes flying off me.

The anger fuels me and I get up, my heart pounding and my face feeling hot. Lisa scrambles up and is staring at me as is everyone in the room. "You decide right now," I say, my voice loud. "Are you going to help us or not? Are you going to fight her or not? Are you going to create a life worth living down here or are you going to fold under and accept Talia's cruelty for the rest of what promises to be your very short lives?"

Lisa is standing there half-crouched for a moment with the knife still in her hand. The room is quiet and everyone's hearts are beating hard. I can't hear their hearts but I can sense them. It's a bit disconcerting, the overlay of the zombie senses the fungus my body is fighting has granted me.

There are no guns drawn and we aren't far from that, but Lisa straightens up and smiles. "That was good, Woody," she says. "But when it's Talia, go for the throat or something more vulnerable. Fight dirty. She will."

I stand there blinking as my brain gets into gear and I realize what is going on. This was a test, but not just Lisa's test. My face flushes hot, and I turn and see that June has a sheepish look on her face as does Dallas. They were in on it.

I turn to Wade and say, "Get Talia on the radio." I walk out of the dining hall without looking back.

CHAPTER THREE

LIKE MOST BUILDINGS at Phantom Ranch, the mule barn is built from wood and local rock. It's got a low roof with a shallow pitch and comprises one end of a large circular corral.

I groan as I follow Wade to it. This is my second time to Phantom Ranch post-apocalypse and I was here a couple of times pre, but I never saw this up close.

The corral is bigger and better built than the one Dallas and I just endured, with a lovely mesquite tree planted in the center, but the similarity is disturbing.

The corral is not far from the Colorado, and while I can't see the river, I can hear it, smell it, and feel a slight increase in humidity, the air not quite so dry.

The barn is built in five segments on the west side of the corral. The two end segments are enclosed squares and the three in the middle are open.

The structure is clearly old and at once feels like it belongs to a past century—which it does—and fits right into the current era. It's simple and rough and will last a long time with minimal care.

"Did you know?" I ask Wade as we walk through the dusty, smelly dirt of the corral.

"Know what?" he asks, his voice a low mumble which I am coming to know is just the way he talks.

"Lisa's little test back in the dining hall," I say. I'm still mad about it and figure the steroids are coloring my reaction.

"Yes," he says.

I stop near the tree in the middle. It's surrounded by a rock wall, presumably to keep the mules away. There is one mule standing in the shade of the corral and staring at us.

"And did I pass?" I ask.

Wade turns and looks at me, his grey eyes looking even sadder. He glances at his watch. "We only have a minute until their next call, maybe we can talk about this later. In the interest of full disclosure, I will be recording the conversation for further analysis."

"Did I pass?" I ask, putting Wade deeper into the geek column after that little speech.

"Yes," he says without emotion. "Let's see if you pass this next test."

He turns around and walks into the square structure through an aged wooden door with faded dark brown paint. I see one solar panel on the shingled roof and a few large antennae.

At first it's dark inside but he flips on a switch, and while the room smells like old, stale hay, it's full of gear. A short-wave radio, a bank of 12-volt car batteries, a crude workbench with four different drones sitting on it, high-end walkie-talkies nestled in their chargers that look to have custom wiring, and a neat arrangement of tubs and bins that must contain a treasure trove of old tech.

It took a lot of time and energy to get all of this down here. When we were last here, a couple of weeks ago, I saw no sign of intelligent usage of tech. Talia put a lot of effort into this, a clear sign of her intentions regarding Phantom Ranch.

It's hot and stuffy but I love this little room. I would never classify myself a geek, but I have found a lot of joy in hacking technology.

No sooner are we in there than one of the walkie-talkies crackles to life. "Phantom Company, this is Striking Eagle, are you there?

Please acknowledge. Over." It's a man, but I don't recognize the voice.

Wade grabs the walkie from the bench and hands it to me. He pulls out an old cell phone from his pocket and fiddles with it, starting a recording, I presume.

"Phantom Company, Striking Eagle. Acknowledge. Over."

"This will go on for a bit if you need a moment," Wade says.

I don't like the way he says it, like I might not be ready, like he is emphasizing that this is another test.

I press the button on the walkie and say, "Beckman here. Can you get Talia for me? Pretty please? Over."

Wade's face quirks into a smile when I say "pretty please" and he pushes back his curly black hair from his forehead.

There's a pause of about a minute and I feel my stomach tighten, so I close my eyes and feel for Talia through the zombie group mind mesh network.

She's alone, there's one other living near her but not too close. I smile because I figure I interrupted her taking a dump. There are pit toilets at Indian Gardens and at this point in the apocalypse, especially if you actually have some TP, they are quite the luxury.

Think about it. I know I say "Any _____ in an apocalypse" a lot. But "Any working toilet in an apocalypse" is the real deal. Because there aren't that many working toilets anymore. No water pressure, no flushing, and if you can't flush the ubiquitous porcelain toilet, it's no use at all.

Sure, pit toilets tend to stink, but it's better than being out in the open, your butt hanging over a hole you just dug, squatting uncomfortably. It's not like diets are properly balanced these days and you can expect the proceedings to be quick and to the point. So, yeah, a pit toilet, smelly though it may be, is a hell of a luxury.

As I stand there, a weird grin on my face, I imagine that Talia saved it for hours on the trail today knowing there was a pit toilet coming and I couldn't be happier that I am interrupting her personal time.

"Striking Eagle, this is Beckman," I say into the walkie. "Cat got your tongue? Over."

Another long pause and I say into the walkie, "Okay, I've got better things to do. You all take your time getting down here, let us get our surprises ready. Over and out."

When I open my eyes, Wade has this worried look on his face. I hand him the walkie-talkie and start opening the bins. The first one is small and has a stash of smart phones and charging cables.

"What are you doing?" Wade asks.

I know what he's asking, but I answer the obvious question instead. "Checking out the supplies."

"No," he says, his mumble rising to a normal volume. "With Talia?"

"Playing hard to get," I say, digging into another bin. It's got a jumble of things, a few toy RC trucks, a couple of car alternators, a big tangled wad of wire.

"But... she..." he stammers.

"Look, Wade," I say, closing the bin and turning to him. "She expects everyone to jump at her call, to do everything she asks immediately and perfectly. I need her angry. I need her to not be in control for once."

"There's a lot on the line here," he says.

"No shit," I say back.

"June..." he begins, his grey eyes flicking to the north and Phantom Ranch, a worried look on his face. "She made a deal with me. I... I need this to work."

"What deal?" I ask.

"My... my family," he says, really mumbling this time. "Talia has my family. My wife. My daughters. June said if I helped, you all would go rescue them."

This is news to me. June and I haven't had much time to talk. She did tell me that I had to pretend that Wade and the two beefy boys were not helping if it came up with Talia, but nothing else. But I did sense that confrontation down here, the one that seemed to change the tide. Cleary Wade is intelligent and he appears to be better with tech than I am, so he's valuable and I can easily see that someone like Talia would resort to crude leverage to secure his cooperation.

"And we will," I say. "But one step at a time, okay?"

He swallows and nods.

"What are your girls' names?" I ask.

He's staring at me like he's not sure if I'm real. Being under the not-so-gentle hand of Talia for even the short time he has been and it's not hard to figure out why. The apocalypse caused a sharp drop in empathy. When everyone is in the shit, it's hard to find the energy to care about someone else's problems. But if Phantom Ranch is to work, if we are to start embracing civilization again, that's exactly what we have to do.

"Umm..." he says, adjusting his glasses. "Alison, she's ten and the oldest. And Jessica who is seven."

"You've done a good job keeping your family safe," I say, and I mean it. I failed those I considered family in Phoenix and I'm dedicated to not doing it again.

"It's been...." he says, shaking his head, those sad grey eyes looking even sadder. Wade with his knowledge and skill is a valuable commodity these days, and I'm sure he's been passed around from psychotic, petty, wannabe warlord to psychotic, petty, wannabe warlord.

"I know," I say gently. "I take it you were with Brown before." Brown was the psychotic, petty, wannabe warlord that led the Flagstaff gang before Talia.

Wade nods, his eyes not meeting mine. "Briefly," he says. "We were in Las Vegas before that and... well... let's just say there are a lot of people like Talia. We barely got away, and now..." He ends in a sad sigh.

I find myself liking the guy. Maybe it's knowing that he has a family that he loves deeply. Maybe it's realizing that he's been through a lot just like the rest of us since the Zs came. Whatever it is, he's suddenly more human.

"So, let's take care of Talia," I say. "And then we can go get your family and bring them down here."

"Really?" he asks.

I nod and smile and this time it feels like a genuine smile. "All we have to do is survive."

Despite the steroids, despite the trauma of the last few weeks, I feel this flicker of hope. Not necessarily hope for my own future— there is still Talia to contend with and the seemingly inevitable conclusion of this fungal infection—but hope for humankind. Maybe there are other pockets of survivors that have found a good place and are trying to throw off the tyranny of the psychotic, petty, wannabe warlords. Maybe there is hope for us yet.

CHAPTER FOUR

I DON'T DWELL on the hope. I've written about that plenty already, about how despair is waiting behind every dashed hope. But I do dwell on the sense of humanity and what might be the spark of a friendship between Wade and me.

There's a couple of folding chairs in the dim mule barn and we sit and chat. Not about the hard things we've all been through but about the simple joys of the before times.

Wade was a software engineer and tinkered with hardware on the side. He knows all about the Arduino microcontroller and even has some down here and a few Raspberry Pi single-board computers. This is the kind of stuff that Q, the guy that taught me about hacking the apocalypse in Phoenix, loved. It's nice to talk about it and it's also sad because of how things ended in Phoenix.

I rattle on about baseball and how I used to love to sit in a stadium watching a game. I get that people thought baseball could be kind of slow, but I think that's because they didn't really get the game. It wasn't about how many runs a team brought home, but about the constant battle between pitcher and batter, about the scramble of the rest of the team when someone did get a hit, about the mental game that drove the physical performance.

We have been on the run so long that just having a conversation with another human being was a balm to me. My sense of the zombie group mind is still there, but it fades. The steroids are still coursing through my veins and I probably laugh too loud on the occasions that laughter is appropriate, but it's a really nice few minutes until the radio comes to life.

"Mr. Woodpecker," Talia says on the walkie-talkie, the pleasant lilt of her southern accent undone by the sneer in her voice. "Did I hear that you are, by some miracle, still alive?"

Talia doesn't do "over" or any of the other radio protocols. It's a little thing but it drives me nuts. She was military. She was trained in this stuff. But it seems she thinks herself so important that this just doesn't matter.

Wade gets up and hands me the walkie, holding it gingerly like it might shock him or something. He pulls his phone out and fiddles with it again, getting the recording going.

"The day I die will be a sad day for you," I say, also disregarding the protocols. If she's not going to do it, I'm not.

"And why is that?" Talia asks.

"I give purpose to your life, Talia," I say. "You would be sad and unfulfilled if you couldn't spend your days torturing me."

She chuckles into the walkie and it sounds more than a little bit psychotic, Wade stares at the walkie with his eyes wide. "Plenty of other fish, you know," she says.

"And," I say, "I'll admit you've certainly given my life a certain amount of shape and meaning. Without you, I doubt that June and I would be together. In many ways, you cemented the relationship, and I guess I have to thank you for that. I can't say that I will miss you when you're dead, but I will feel your absence."

There's a pause and then she says, "Tell me, Mr. Woodpecker, do you know something I don't?"

"There are certainly things I know that you don't, Talia," I say. "But there are some things I know that you know. Like you and your troops, numbered around thirty-five, are currently stopped at Indian Gardens."

I stop short of telling her that I know about the people hiking down from the North Rim or that I know her group has precisely forty-three people in it. And I'm certainly tempted to bring up her recent personal time, but that would be going too far.

She doesn't answer and I have to shove down the impulse to keep needling her. I need her mad but not too mad.

When Talia comes back on the radio, her tone is an icy-cold fury. "You tell that Wade Goodwin that when I seem him, I'm gonna break his neck myself. And when I get back to Flagstaff, I'm gonna pull his family apart limb by limb."

Wade is white as a sheet and staring at me wide-eyed.

"Not sure who you are talking about," I say. "June, bless her heart, saw fit to take a few prisoners during what happened down here. Maybe this Wade is one of them. In any case, it didn't take long to find the fine stash of drones. You can't make a move that I won't know about."

There's another silence, but this one brief. "What the hell do you want, Woodpecker?"

"I want you to keep your date with me," I say. "Just you and maybe a second. Let your men take a good rest up at Indian Gardens. We can turn this into a proper duel. On the Bright Angel Suspension Bridge like we first agreed."

She laughs and it comes out tinny from the walkie-talkie and breaks up a little. "Why the hell would I do that?"

"If you are afraid I'll win," I say, "well then, we don't have to do it that way. We'll just pick you off one by one when you all are coming down the inner gorge."

It's certainly not that simple. If they wait until after dark there wouldn't be much we could do. And even during the day it would be a fight with plenty of cover available.

Talia is silent again so I ask Wade, "Is there enough dynamite down here to blow the bridges?"

He shakes his head and says, "All that was left was on that vest."

That's three sticks. Placed properly you might be able to blow one bridge but not both, and even if the bridges are blown, the river is swimmable here. This is June's area, not mine, but I have to wonder how you defend this place from a determined foe. Its remoteness does help, for sure, but I don't know if it's enough.

Talia comes back on the walkie and says, "How do I know you won't just pick me off when I come down the trail?" she asks.

"You have my word," I say.

She laughs long and hard, the tinny nature of the speakers making it sound more psychotic than it actually is. And I get her doubt. She thinks everyone is like she is. When she let Dallas and me go near the North Rim, it was only to release us into a situation where we had slim odds of survival. She obeyed the letter of her agreement but not the spirit.

When she finally stops laughing, I say, "Clearly you aren't up to it. That is so disappointing."

"And clearly you all aren't up to this battle," she counters. "Why else would you challenge me to a fight you can't possibly win?"

She had me there, at least on the delaying tactic part. And while I know my chances of defeating her in a fight are slim, there is still a chance. She is acting more like the classic bully than I had thought she would, backing down from a direct challenge. Only wanting a confrontation if the odds are stacked in her favor.

"Suit yourself," I say, trying to sound as casual as I can. "I just can't wait to see everyone's faces when they hear you chickened out."

I know. That's a really childish thing to say. I don't expect her to act like Marty McFly in the *Back to the Future* movies and take the stupidest of challenges just because someone called her a chicken.

She chuckles, and it's an evil sound. "Tell you what, Mr. Woodpecker. Just because I'm fond of some of the folks down there and I'd like to avoid excess bloodshed, I'll make you a deal. I'll leave most of the boys and just ten of us will come down. You pick nine of the best down there and we'll meet at that lovely little corral where you found Miss Dallas.

"If I win, everyone down there surrenders. If you win..." she chuckles again. "If by some miracle Jesus and Gaia bless you with abilities you just don't have, well then I'll be dead and I just don't give a damn what you do."

"When I win," I say into the walkie. "Your troops will leave and never come back."

She snorts. "Sure. Why not? If you are going to live in a fantasy world, Mr. Woodpecker, you might as well really go for it." She then laughs for a good long time while Wade stares at me wide-eyed.

CHAPTER FIVE

BACK IN THE dining hall everyone is huddled around one of the long wooden tables as Wade plays the recording of the call. I hate every second of it. I think of how I could have done better. I hate hearing my voice through the recording sounding very different to how I sound to myself.

While it's playing, Lisa is busy signing the contents of the conversation to Milo and Ralph so it seems my shame is being communicated through multiple languages.

"All you had to do was call her chicken?" Lisa asks when the recording is over.

I just shrug.

June shakes her head and says, "This way she gets nine armed men and herself into the middle of camp." She looks at me. "What's the latest intel?"

"The south group is moving again," I say. "And the north group never stopped."

"We're screwed," Meryl says.

"Unless you beat her," Dallas offers.

Milo taps Lisa on the shoulder and starts signing. I feel bad about just calling these guys "beefy boys." I get that we dehumanize our enemies, but he's not an enemy now so he feels more human, but nothing essential changed except the side he has aligned himself with.

And while Milo and his brother Ralph do look similar, are built like linebackers, have square faces and brown eyes, they are quite different. Milo smiles a lot more than Ralph and has his brown hair just long enough for some wave to show.

Lisa nods and says, "Milo says that even if Talia dies they won't stop. This place is too big a prize. If you manage to beat her, that just means the shooting will start right then and there."

Meryl crosses his arms and asks, "Well, what do we do then?"

Lisa looks right at me. She's across the table from me this time, so unless she's a ninja I don't think I'll end up flat on my back on the floor. "There's still that raft," she says, her eyes intense. She then looks at June and Dallas. "You guys can get out of here. She'll chase you."

"But not before she cleans house," June says.

Lisa shrugs. "So you tie some of us up before you go."

"People will talk," Dallas says. "Talia will apply enough pressure and people will talk. And then all of you will end up in the zombie pen with Harris."

Lisa nods and stares down at the wooden table and everyone else is silent.

This is the apocalypse, you constantly face impossible problems and impossible choices.

The moments tick by, the room hot and the air still, the silence too deep until Milo bangs on the table and starts signing to Lisa.

"He says," she begins, nodding and swallowing hard. "He says, 'Then we fight like we have nothing to lose.'" Lisa looks at us all, searching our faces. "Because we don't have anything to lose."

Everyone is silent again, the moments awkward and stilted, until Ralph slaps his brother on the back and gives a thumbs-up and a wicked grin.

Ralph signs and Lisa translates. "And we make sure Talia pays for what she has done to us."

There are shouts, and Lisa, Milo, and Ralph bang on the table, but I am not feeling it. I smile and pump my fist, but I can't mask my worry. All this time running from Talia and just trying to survive was one thing—going to war with her is something completely different.

We all kill Zs, there is no choice, but can we all kill the living? Can I pull the trigger or swing the bat when it's a living, breathing human being?

And what about the Zs that are poised to attack? How the hell can we handle them, especially if the fight at the mule corral happens and Talia's people are in the middle of Phantom Ranch?

When things die down and the planning starts, I go to June and Dallas and say, "We need to talk."

CHAPTER SIX

JUNE, Dallas, and I are down by Bright Angel Creek, the burble of it and the moist air a relief even though the sun is hot. We're south of the dining hall a little in sight of the zombie pen, the four of them snarling, straining, and reaching for us, their fetid bouquet assaulting my nose. The Phantom Ranch survivors are still in the dining hall getting ready to go to war with Talia.

It wasn't easy to get Dallas here, she can't put any weight on her right foot and we are off the trail, the area near the creek littered with stones. She looks exhausted and is leaning heavily on her cane with a sour look on her face and asks, "What is it? Why the hell did you have to drag me out here?"

I bite my lip and nod towards the Zs. The steroids have made the zombie group mind a little more distant but it is still there, and being this close to them, looking at them, is a little like being in a hall of mirrors. I can see them, but I can also sense them sensing me. I feel their hunger and their need. I feel Harris's anger, whatever is left of him, desperate to get out, to get to Talia.

"Watch them," I say and close my eyes.

It's better with my eyes closed, no hall of mirrors. I'm aware of all the living and all the Zs in the area. Someone has followed us from the dining hall and is watching us from a nearby cottonwood. I'm not sure because I don't know her well enough, but I'm pretty sure it's Lisa.

I ignore the living and focus on the four Zs in the pen. I feel their hunger and their need, but I fill them up with my own need, a simple need, a need for quiet.

They resist at first, like children fighting sleep, but my mind is stronger than theirs are. With my eyes still closed, I whisper, "Now" and they go quiet.

"Shiiiit..." Dallas intones.

"You can..." June whispers. "You can control them?"

I open my eyes, letting go of the effort, and take off my baseball cap and wipe the sweat from my forehead. "Kind of. Some of them, but I have no idea to what extent."

They are both staring at me so I explain what I did with the Zs that were in Sal and Mary's path hiking out from the river when we took the raft. About how, hanging there with Dallas, I fought with some of the desiccated ones and stopped the Zs from attacking Phantom Ranch.

"Desiccated ones" is a weird term, but I'm not sure how else to quickly indicate the Zs that I've seen at the center of pods, the ones that seem to be the key to them being more intelligent. They are more mature, in zombie terms, and all dried out—they are literally desiccated.

Calling them leaders would be a little bit misleading because it really is a group mind in the end, but the desiccated ones do exert more influence.

"We can't tell anyone," Dallas says, looking around. "No one. Not ever."

June nods and bites her lip. "Some will embrace it, especially while this new thing you can do is useful, but after that...? You'll be lucky if you are treated like a leper and only banished."

I nod. I get it. I'm not even comfortable with what is happening to me. While the long-sleeve shirt I am wearing is hot and the half-gloves are awkward, I'm glad that June had the foresight to have me don them before we got here.

"But how do we do this and keep it a secret?" I ask.

June brushes at her short black hair with her hand, sighs, closes her eyes, and tilts her head to the sun. God, she's beautiful, her olive skin welcoming the sun whereas mine just gets burned.

I know she's thinking, trying to find a moment of peace in this mad, mad day. I need a moment too, but instead of closing my eyes, I stare at her round face, her delicate nose, her lovely cheekbones.

Dallas, surprisingly, is quiet too, her gaze going from June to me and back to June. The creek gurgles and I hear distant voices as someone has a conversation under the cottonwood trees.

With a sigh, June opens up her eyes, the ocean blue of them completing the picture of beauty that is her face. She nods and licks her lips. "The odds are shit," she says, "but I have a plan. We let Talia in with her men. You will lose the fight, and while you're down, you'll call in your army of Zs."

There's clearly more to it, but even that brief outline leaves me cold in the hot sun. But I don't say anything. I'm the crazy man that challenged Talia in the first place. Sure, I was trying to save Dallas's life since she had just been captured, and that has kind of worked out, but it doesn't make it any less crazy.

"This is absolutely crazy," Dallas says, echoing my thoughts.

June shrugs. "There was this soldier I've read about, named Stockdale. He was captured in Vietnam, spent seven years in a prison camp and it didn't break him. There's something called the 'Stockdale Paradox.' You have to both confront the brutal facts of your situation and have unwavering faith that you will prevail in the end."

"The facts are certainly brutal," I offer.

"And if we don't prevail," Dallas says with a cheerful smile, "we'll be dead, so... you know..."

The three of us stand there for a few moments staring at each other and I am once again reminded how lucky I am not to be a go-it-alone survivor anymore and to have these two amazing women in my life.

"Okay," I say with a nod. "There's some timing issues. The Zs upstream will take some time to get here."

June nods, "We can deal with that."

"And I don't know how well I can control them," I say.

"Well you best get to practicing," Dallas offers.

"And we're being watched," I say. "Don't look, but they're to the northeast behind a cottonwood. Someone followed us from the dining hall. I think it's Lisa."

"Well," Dallas says cheerfully. "We better make out then."

My jaw drops and Dallas adds, "It's what they are all thinking. Everyone can see you drooling over June, and after what you just did to save me, well..." she ends in a shrug.

June has a smile playing on her lips. There's more here and Dallas hinted at it in the corral when she was a bomb and I was trying to figure out how to play Talia's game and save her life. Apparently June and Dallas talked while I was unconscious fighting the zombie infection from all those scratches I got in Winslow.

June laughs. It's a light, happy sound. "I love it when he blinks that much."

Dallas shrugs and says, "I guess he's not ready. You better kiss him. God knows someone should get kissed around here."

"Well this is going to really make him blink," June says and grabs Dallas, pulls her head down, and kisses her hard.

Dallas squeals briefly, clearly surprised, but then melts into the kiss.

June was right, it does make me blink. A lot. My fevered brain trying to figure it out, my exhausted body more than a little bit intrigued.

They don't kiss that long, but then June grabs me and kisses me. Hard. I grab her and kiss her back and that strange and complicated hunger I feel for her with the zombie group mind is redoubled. Passion is definitely a hunger, and even before the infection I felt like

I wanted to eat June up, metaphorically of course. With the influence of the zombie mind it's, very weirdly, less metaphorical.

I hold back just a little, because literally eating her would be a very bad thing, but it is still so intense, infused with my own longing for her and the Zs' group hunger.

When we part, June wipes away the moisture on her lips and is blinking a lot herself and says, "Woody... that...."

Dallas sighs. "It's true love. I get that, guys. No need to rub it in."

June is still staring at me and I can see real hunger in her eyes. She liked it and I feel my face flushing red because it wasn't all me.

"And you two clearly need a room again," Dallas says.

I clear my throat and say, "That's not exactly safe right now."

Dallas felt this energy when we were just trussed up hanging above the corral just a few hours ago. "Oh..." she says. "Yeah." She turns to June. "We have to worry about him getting a little bitey now, what with his friends whispering in his ear." She nods towards the zombie pen where the four of them are snarling and reaching for us.

June's cheeks, even though her skin is olive-toned, flash just a little bit red. "That's interesting."

So Dallas seems to want a throuple and June is intrigued about the idea of sex with me under the influence of the zombie group mind. All of this while we are preparing to go to war with Talia and her little army, the first battle being me taking on Talia hand-to-hand.

Not to mention the fungal infection that I'm currently fighting that is likely to end me soon.

Yup, this is my life.

Say what you will about the difficulties of the apocalypse, but you sure as hell can't call it boring.

CHAPTER SEVEN

I LEAVE the war-room planning to June, Dallas, and the rest of them. Earlier, by the gurgling creek after some highly awkward and strangely charged moments, June outlined her plan further. It's enough for me. I don't need to be involved in the fine detail and logistical planning, of which there is a lot and not that many hours.

Talia and company, the group coming down from the South Rim, will be here around sunset if they keep up their pace. The North Rim group will be a bit later—they have farther to go but are moving a little bit faster.

I find a big cottonwood tree outside the dining hall and sit against the rough bark and close my eyes. I'm not trying to nap, the steroids won't let me. I'm doing as Dallas suggested and am attempting to "practice" so I can control, as June put it, "my army of Zs."

As if.

This is a group mind which means there's a chance that they will control me not the other way around. Control is not even the right word here—it's more like influence.

I hear voices rise in the dining hall, Dallas and Lisa in particular and, surprisingly, the soft-spoken Meryl. They are clearly having a heated discussion about the upcoming madness and trying to come to a workable consensus.

With the zombie group mind, it's more like that. The mission of the Zs is clear. It's the same mission as those around that table in the Phantom Ranch dining hall. Survival. But just like those in the dining hall, it's not always clear what the best way to go about it is and there is often disagreement.

The desiccated ones hold more sway in the Zs' discussion just as I seem to. Inside, I suspect that June and the rest of them with military training hold more sway in that particular discussion.

And, yes, I got the Zs in the pen to be quiet on command. But that was only four Zs and it was hard. I can't do that with hundreds of them. I have to find a way for our needs to align. Their need to survive and our need to survive.

As I tap into the group mind, I feel all the living and the kinda dead here in Phantom Ranch. I start with the four Zs in the pen. I don't try to make them be quiet, I just suggest to them that they need to save their energy for later. I show them the group of humans to the south getting closer. I impress upon them that Talia is there.

And they don't get quiet. They shamble to the south side of the pen, their arms reaching towards where Talia is, and get louder. Much louder.

Zombies are children.

I reach out to the desiccated ones, the three of them that are at the center of the pods. One in The Box to the north, and two with the groups staged by the Colorado River upstream to the east.

I don't try to influence them or project my wants and needs, I just try to feel where they are at. I've described the zombie group mind as something of a mesh network, and it's an apt metaphor. Each Z has a limited range of its fresh brains radar and in terms of being able to communicate with other Zs, but because they are properly spaced out, I can check in with the desiccated ones.

Kind of like when we had an internet and you could ping an

address across the world and it would go from node to node to node until it got to its destination.

Now Zs are the only real internet left. At least these Zs that are forming this network in the Grand Canyon. And they did it, unfortunately, in an expressed effort to eat the living at Phantom Ranch.

But I'm getting distracted here. I mean it is distracting because the one thing I can feel without a doubt or any equivocation is their immense hunger. And that's the first thing I get when I check in with the desiccated ones, unrelenting hunger. And then impatience edging towards desperation.

They are desperately trying to survive, which, I think, is a very good reason to only classify them as kind-of-dead. The revelations about the Harris Z and his (its) latent fury at Talia is further blurring the line between living and Z.

So, I sense hunger. Desperation. The need to survive. And one more thing. Fear.

When I got them to stop their attack as I hung with Dallas above the corral, I had filled the network with idealized images of well-armed living easily defeating Zs. The living armed with automatic weapons and grenade launchers, the images informed by my time playing video games. Apparently those images took hold and the group mind is trying to figure out how to succeed. They want to know how to defeat well-armed humans and get the meal they so desperately need.

And they are desperate. The zombies just recently started forming what we are calling pods. With the desiccated ones at the center of them, they are no longer unthinking, unwavering hunger incarnate, but they are strategizing, thinking, unwavering hunger incarnate.

They got smart just in time to figure out they don't have forever to find a meal. And with the creation of the mesh network, they know there is only one meal in town and that is down here at Phantom Ranch.

Except there isn't just the only meal anymore. There are the groups coming down from the North and South Rims.

And this is June's plan. Let the Zs have Talia's people. Hold them off until the time is right and let them feast.

But these are the living we are talking about. People that have (or had) families. People that have banded together in a desperate bid for survival. People who, just like me, want to get through the day and find a little joy.

And these people are our enemies and this is war.

I sit there under the tree with my eyes closed, a war going on in my own mind. The Zs will attack Phantom Ranch at some point. I haven't seen it yet, but I am convinced that Zs will eventually "die" if they go without nutrition long enough, and they know we are here so they will try.

And Talia's troops will attack, or at least take over Phantom Ranch, regardless of the outcome of our fight.

And there are the survivors here who just want to live in peace but are being forced to fight to defend what they have.

These three factions are heading for inevitable conflict and death is sure to follow.

There seems to be no choice. I need to help the Zs come up with a plan to succeed against Talia's people, because while the Zs are growing more intelligent, they don't have firearms and the survivors down here will have a much easier time with them than with Talia's little army.

I hate to do it, but sitting under that cottonwood tree, I enter the discussion.

CHAPTER EIGHT

"WAKE UP, WOODY."

The voice comes from a great distance away floating into the chaos that is my mind. Well, it's not just my mind anymore. It's the mind of 267 Zs and me. It's the group mind of the Grand Canyon zombie population, at least those within range, and me.

It is chaos, but it's more than just that. There are primitive presences that do the equivalent of shout all the time. Simple concepts like "hungry," "need to eat," "must feed." Those voices are just the background noise of the group mind, the insatiable never-ending hunger that is part of it, almost like it's the carrier signal of the group mind.

And then there are more developed voices that express their needs more subtly and consider not just the immediate need to feed, but what happens when they try to feed and question if they will survive long enough to feed.

Then there are some still more sophisticated voices that wonder what happens after they feed. Where will the next meal come from? How will they survive long term? How will they increase their numbers?

There are other side discussions, like not focusing on humans and trying to eat animals to survive, but there is a general distaste for it like they know it is enough for survival but it is somehow "wrong." There is also the matter that healthy animals can easily escape them in most cases.

"Do you think he's..." another voice says. The voices are both female and familiar, but I am really in the group mind now and I can't pay attention to them.

There are no words being said in the Z-mind—that is not how things are communicated. It's simpler than words and more primitive. It's almost like the ideas and discussion is happening at a deeper level where words are not needed.

Those more sophisticated voices are the desiccated ones. I was wrong before, there are not three of them, one with each group, but a dozen of them spread across the canyon. With me there are thirteen what I would call developed minds involved in the discussion.

Except, it's not like any discussion I've ever had. It's more like a mental wrestling match with the more primitive minds piling on to whatever concept feels right to them.

I hope this makes sense. The words are very hard to find because what we are doing has no words.

"No," the first voice says. "He's still alive. I can see his carotid artery pulsing."

"They'll be here in a couple hours," the second voice says. "Wade sent up a drone. Talia's full force is heading down towards the river at Pipe Creek. And we have no idea what's going on up the Kaibab Trail. We need him."

"I know, Dallas," the first voice says. "Just give us a few minutes."

The wrestling of the minds is, at least from my perspective, almost subconscious. I am part of it, to be sure, but I'm not thinking in words or considering what I am putting into the group mind, I am just a node in the mind and my experiences and biases are directly guiding my participation.

I'm no longer trying to be part of the group mind, I just am. And the 268 of us (the Zs and me) are not of one mind. Not by a long shot.

But I am dimly aware that I have made progress, but the thin part of me that can worry about such things, very much worries about the cost.

You see, I am helping the Zs, the Z-mind, at least this one, get smarter. I have a meat brain still, not a fungus brain. Well... I'm pretty sure my brain is still mostly meat. Clearly there is enough fungus in me to make me a node in the zombie mesh network. My mostly meat brain has better cognition than all the other minds in the network, and at this point it's almost like my mind is being used for its processing power.

Scenarios flicker through my brain for me to evaluate, ways that the Zs can get what they need and survive against the armed forces that are heading towards them.

And since most of this is below conscious control, I have no choice but to evaluate them and send the results back to the Z-mind. It's usually images, like I tried with them when I was stopping the attack earlier in the day. But sometimes it's a simple one-word equivalent, like "no." Or a little more verbose, something like, "we all die."

"Woody?" the first voice says, this time it's a whisper. "Are you still with me? Please still be with me. I need you. I know I ran off and got us into this mess. I know I put the fight with Talia first. But I don't want to be in this world without you."

It's not her words that get to me so much as the tone and a single thought floats through my mind, "June."

"When we met," she says, "I knew you were different. At the dog food factory when I was on the roof and you were trapped on that semitrailer surrounded by Zs, you were joking with me. Everyone else I met was dead serious, focused on only one thing. Survival. But every day you try to make sure we laugh, that we feel something else besides the weight of survival."

June's words are calling to me, but it's not enough. I've been describing the zombie group mind in internet terms and to stretch that analogy a little further, what is going on with me now is like a denial of service attack. I have so much coming at me via the group mind, that I have lost control over part of my brain. I am not quite conscious anymore.

"Woody," she says. "I need you. Not just for this fight or the next fight, but for after the fights are all over and we have to figure out a way to be human, a way to be civilized, a way to be happy."

She takes my hand and I suck in a breath. It's not voluntary at all. Being touched after being locked into the flow of the group mind reaches me on a deeper level.

"Woody," June says as she squeezes my hand. "Please!"

I hear desperation in her voice and that reaches me a little more and I am able to refuse some of what is coming to me through the group mind, like the beginnings of a firewall against the denial of service attack.

"I love you, Woody Beckman," she says with a sniff.

That reaches me even more and I try to speak but it just comes out as a groan.

"I'm sorry about this," she says, and then she slaps me. Hard.

Fiery pain blossoms in my left cheek and my head rocks to the side, grating painfully against the rough bark of the cottonwood tree I'm leaning against.

"Hey!" I say, putting my hand to my stinging cheek. I wasn't trying to say anything, it just came out. This slap thing was becoming something of a pattern. Dallas slapped me a few days ago after June left us and I couldn't make a decision.

My eyes fly open, and I see the lovely round face of June Medina and the tears that are on her cheeks.

The Z-mind is still with me, it's still part of me, but now it's running in the background. I can feel it, like whispered words that I can't quite understand, but at least I am conscious.

"Sorry about that," she says.

I grab her and hug her hard and say, "I love you too."

CHAPTER NINE

THE NEXT FEW hours are sheer madness. We've all long ago left exhaustion behind and are all shambling around on sheer will.

And, yes, I used the word "shambling" above on purpose. At one point, I am with Meryl packing some backpacks with foodstuffs in the kitchen of the dining hall and look up as a woman named Grace comes stumbling in and looks around confused.

She's got long blond hair that was in a ponytail, but much of the hair has escaped, haloing her forlorn face, her eyes not quite focusing.

"Over here, Grace," Meryl says gently, and she stumbles forward and looks just like a Z, except for the lack of yellow eyes and the snarling.

She takes the backpack from Meryl and wanders off.

Grace and most of the other "civilians" are evacuating Phantom Ranch. No one is really a civilian anymore, not now, but some are more suited to what is coming than others. It's a spectrum, really. I often think that June is more prepared for this than I am with her military training and her physical fitness. But that's just silly. No one, except the psychotic, petty, wannabe warlords are really suited for this time. It's hard on all of us.

"You okay, Woody?" Meryl asks.

The kitchen isn't that big, with the same wooden walls and floor as the dining hall with a big gas range, a fridge that is now used for storage, some stainless-steel tables and sinks, and a bunch of steel cabinets.

Even without the Grateful Dead T-shirt, Meryl with his grey beard, glasses, and kind face looks like a deadhead. We've been putting little baggies of weed in with the food. I haven't seen it, but they must be growing some down here.

I nod. "Yeah," I say. "Just one of those days that seem to last a year."

He smiles and nods. We've all had them since it went to shit. "You sure you want to do this?" he asks.

He's talking about facing Talia. I shake my head. "Of course not," I say. "She's going to kick my ass."

Meryl's eyes widen as if he's surprised I knew that. "Then why?" he asks.

I nod toward where Grace just stumbled out. "We're buying you all some time." Meryl will be evacuating too, and I'm glad of it. Actually, I'm glad Phantom Ranch has "civilians" to evacuate.

Talia treated this place like it was her own platoon, calling it Phantom Company, but it was mostly full of regular people that gravitated to the confidence that Talia exuded when the world started falling apart. None of them were expecting the petty and psychotic aspects of her to completely take over.

I can't tell the full truth to Meryl, that I am part of the zombie group mind and this place is likely be full of Zs before it's all over, that I won't likely see him again, that if Talia doesn't get me the fungus probably will, that this isn't quite the sacrifice he thinks, more of me using myself up in the best way possible.

Meryl puts his hand on my arm. "Don't lose yourself," he says with a crooked smile. "In all this shit, don't lose yourself."

I smile and nod. I think he means don't give up who I am just to defeat Talia. It's good advice for the apocalypse. Hell, it was good advice before the Zs came. I hope I can follow it. But today, with the Z-mind, not losing myself takes on a whole different dimension.

"Woody," June calls from the dining hall. "We need an update on the intel. Can you go check in?"

I hold Meryl's gaze for another breath and then say, "I'll do my best."

The older man gives me a small smile and a nod. "I know you will." He pauses, his eyes intense behind his glasses. "I'll see you soon, Woody."

CHAPTER TEN

"THERE'S ONLY TEN OF THEM?" June asks for the fifth time.

We're standing on the southern end of the Bright Angel Suspension Bridge behind a metal barricade waiting for Talia and company.

I nod. "The rest of them are out of sight about a mile back where the trail hits the river at Pipe Creek. It's amazing, really."

June bites her lower lip and nods. She shifts from foot to foot as I peer through the slit in the barricade and watch the ten of them approach the bridge.

The trail over there is cut into the hard rock of the cliff, and the ten of them are extremely exposed. I'm sure while I was locked in the Z-mind there were discussions of taking them out at a distance, but I don't think June would have agreed to that.

This is all very complicated for her.

The Bright Angel Bridge is often called the Silver Bridge because of the plain steel used to construct it. It's narrow with high railings on either side and a metal grate bottom that lets you see the river rushing by about sixty feet below you.

It was built in the late sixties and was key to the creation of the Transcanyon Waterline that pumped water from Roaring Springs near the North Rim up to the South Rim. Not that that matters anymore, but trivia can be a comfort to me in tense situations.

Talia's people are clearly well armed with rifles slung over their shoulders and pistols on their belts. But the firearms are all put away and that just makes my stomach tighten.

Not that I want a firefight. But I don't want to face Talia hand-to-hand either. But we are prepared for a firefight on this side with those good with rifles placed at strategic positions behind us with good cover. We would have the upper hand, at least for a few minutes until the rest of Talia's people could get down here.

It feels right that it's only June and me waiting for them. The practical reason is that Talia and her people are unlikely to attack us. June, because in Talia's mind she hasn't suffered enough for her sins yet. Me, because Talia will soon have the opportunity to hit me, repeatedly, in front of an audience which I am sure she is eager to do.

The "civilians" are well on their way up Clear Creek Trail and are hopefully out of sight by now. There are eight others left here with us including Milo, Ralph, and some other non-civilians.

"I have an idea," I say, and June looks at me, her eyes wide like some little kid who is hoping they can get out of something terrible. "It's just a small thing to unbalance her when it's time for the fight."

She nods for me to continue and bites her lip again.

"I... I can't tell you what it is, but I just wanted to warn you that I might say something, and that what I say will be timed to rattle Talia, but it will be real."

Her smooth brow furrows and her eyes narrow. "And you want me to be surprised?"

I nod and feel my face flush. "Yeah."

She shrugs, a quirky smile playing on her thin lips like the thought pleases her. "Okay," she says.

I smile back. It's not much, it's just a small moment, but it is a tiny bit of relief in this madness. Because the fungus is still active in me, I sense her heart rate drop a bit and I smile wider.

"What?" she asks, examining herself like I spotted a bug on her or something.

"I hope you like the surprise," I say. The thought of what I want to do makes my stomach even tighter, and I think of doing it now before things get really tense, but I don't.

Because I'm scared to do it. I'm terrified that she'll—

The ringing sound of footfalls on the metal bridge interrupts the moment and my train of thought. I turn back to the slit in the metal barricade and watch the ten of them stride confidently across the bridge with Talia in the lead.

She's long and lean, taller than me, with her sandy blond hair pulled back into a tight ponytail, the sides of her head shaved. Her jaw is set and her sometimes brown, sometimes hazel eyes show a feral hunger even from a distance.

My stomach tightens even further.

This wood and metal barricade was part of today's work and was made hastily to beef up this position. There's a door cut into it that is bolted in two spots from this side. It won't hold up to a concentrated assault, but it's better than the gate that was here before.

Talia and her people are even more exposed on the bridge. We've got people on the delta upstream a bit with good shots.

"Ready?" I ask June, my tone low.

Her face hardens and she nods.

I open the door and say, "Welcome to Phantom Ranch." I put as much cheerful punch in my voice as I can.

"Welcome to the end of your pitiful little life, Mr. Woodpecker," Talia says with a psychotic smile and her mild southern accent.

CHAPTER ELEVEN

NONE of us say much as we escort Talia and her people into Phantom Ranch. There has been plenty of glaring and posturing, but that is about it. Guns have stayed holstered and rifles have stayed slung on shoulders.

On one hand, I'm stunned that this is happening, that Talia is here, that we are all together and blood hasn't been shed. On the other hand, this is Talia—she is incapable of believing I have any chance of beating her and she must believe that this is an effective way to get what she wants.

The sun is just above the western horizon as we walk along the dusty trail past the main corral where Wade has all the tech stored. There are scraggly mesquite trees and prickly pear cactus here, and the colors of the Bright Angel Canyon darkening as the sun wanes.

The trail is narrow and we are walking single file. I'm in front, followed by Talia, then June, and then the rest of Talia's men.

Past the corral, we walk across a narrow footbridge that spans Bright Angel Creek which burbles cheerfully below us. When we get to the other side, Talia asks, "So why are you doin' this?" Her tone is low, like she doesn't want everyone to hear.

"Letting you beat me to a pulp?" I ask as I continue to walk, my heart thumping in my chest.

"Yeah," she says. "Because you know I will."

"I challenged you to save Dallas," I say.

"Oh, I get that," she says. "You didn't have time and had to come up with an offer I couldn't refuse. Why is this still happenin', is what I wanna know."

"Take a guess," I say.

She chuckles and says, "You've finally realized what an utterly pitiful creature you are and you have decided to use what is left of your life to seein' that I create order around here and ensure we all survive."

I almost stop walking. Does she really think that? Is her narcissistic ego that big? Does she think the fate of the human race is in her hands? Instead, I say, "Something like that."

We fall silent, turn onto North Kaibab Trail, and walk briskly towards Phantom Ranch. I feel the living behind me, I feel the rest of Talia's troops at Pipe Creek, and the group to the north now nearing Ribbon Falls. That puts them about five miles away, maybe an hour and a half if they are really hustling.

That's another reason for this fight from Talia's perspective, to give those troops time to get here.

The Z-mind is more of a part of me now. It's not like I'm telling them what I want them to do, but they can feel what I want just like I can feel what they want. My time locked in the group mind has changed things. Dramatically.

They sense, or rather, we sense the increased number of the living and breathing coming close and our hunger is intensifying.

A few minutes later, we turn a corner and come into view of the old ranger station and, beyond it, the pen with zombie Harris and the other three.

"Well, I'll be," Talia says as we approach, her voice light and cheerful and loud enough for everyone to hear this time. "I was sure you bleedin' hearts would have put them out of their misery by now."

The Zs react to our presence with vigor, snarling and pushing against the pen as well as they can with their broken legs, their arms outstretched.

"Why didn't you blow their heads off, June-bug?" Talia asks.

That nickname grates on my nerves, so I can't imagine what it does to June. I sense her heart speeding up some and I know she just wants to hit Talia, but she doesn't say anything.

Maybe she doesn't trust herself. Maybe she's thinking this will mess with Talia.

"We've been rather busy," I say.

I used to think that Zs had one mode and one volume: hungry and loud. But that's certainly not true, even before they grew a brain. It just so happened that when I usually saw them, they thought they were going to eat so were quite loud.

Zombie Harris and his companions seem to find a new level of frenzy as we approach, their hands reaching for us as they balance as well as they can on their broken legs. Those hands aren't reaching for us collectively, but for Talia specifically.

"Good to see ya too, Harris," she says, her tone poisonous. "You traitorous bastard."

There's some chuckling from Talia's men and more snarling from the Zs as we walk by.

When we arrive at the smaller corral, the one Dallas and I were hanging above earlier today, Talia strides into the center and looks around.

Dallas is there, her face a hard mask, her knuckles white on the gnarled cane she is leaning on. Milo is standing next to her and Ralph and Lisa are on the other side of her, but no one else is here.

"Where is everyone?" Talia asks. "I want an audience for this."

I catch June's eye and she shakes her head. The agreement was that only June and I would speak for this part, but apparently she doesn't want to. Or, more likely, doesn't trust herself.

"They're coming," I say, stepping into the corral. "You'll have an audience, don't worry."

She looks at one of her men, he's taller than her with a narrow face and short blond hair. "They evacuated most of them," Talia says with a nod. "I told ya they would."

He shrugs. "Clear Creek Trail doesn't go anywhere. We'll run them down tomorrow."

Talia turns back to me and asks, "Shall we talk terms?"

"Terms?" I ask.

She nods. "Well, of course, this is a duel."

"Sure..." I say. I know she's going somewhere with this, but I have no idea where.

"Here they are," she says cheerfully. "No weapons of any kind."

I nod. I had expected that.

"No aid will be given by the audience and no aid will be sought by the combatants," she says.

"Fine," I say.

"To prove that neither combatant has any hidden weapons," she says, "no clothing will be worn except for the minimum to preserve dignity."

"You want us to strip down?" I ask.

"Yes, Mr. Woodpecker," she says. "I want to fight you in your tighty-whities. All the better to see you piss yourself."

I have no general objection to that, but, despite the heat of the day, I've been wearing a long-sleeved shirt and half gloves to hide my zombie scratches. You can see them on my wrists where bare skin shows but you'd have to really look to see the white threads of fungus in them. Not so if I take them off.

I look at June and she doesn't meet my gaze, no help there. Dallas's eyes are wide and she bites her lip.

I don't know why, but I notice that Dallas is leaning more towards Milo than Ralph and that Milo keeps glancing down at her. Maybe my brain is just trying to distract me from the inevitable pain that is about to come and my fear of being found out when I take my clothing off. But, no, it's more than that, and maybe it's these fungus-enhanced senses, but there is definitely something there.

Talia must see the hesitation on my face. "Are you afraid?" she asks, and as if to amp up the challenge she pulls her gun and throws it out of the corral to the tall blond man. She starts untying boots, and, right there in front of us all, starts stripping down.

"Fine," I say, but I don't move to take my clothes off yet. On one hand, I don't think it matters if everyone gets a good look at the scratches because my chance of survival is scant. Besides, I hate keeping it a secret.

Talia has her pants off and throws them to the blond man and just stares at me, her arms crossed. Her legs are long and slim but clearly muscular, her toenails are, surprisingly, painted red, and it looks like her pedicure was recent. Must be nice. But what catches my attention are the tattoos. She has tattoos of two snakes, what look like rattlesnakes, winding around her legs with the tails disappearing around her back and the mouths open on her feet.

These snakes on her legs and feet complement the snakes I had already seen tattooed on her arms and feel entirely appropriate to me.

"You got a foot fetish there, Mr. Woodpecker?" she asks.

I shake my head and smile. "No. Just wondering how the hell you have time to take care of your nails."

"I don't," she says, glancing at the tall blond man and looking him up and down.

Was that for June? Is she trying to make her jealous?

Talia looks back at me. "Well?" she says. "I want to see those tighty-whities. Somehow I don't think you're the boxer type."

"We have conditions too," I say.

Talia nods in an exaggerated way and says, "I'm listenin'."

I really do want to just hit her. She's so confident, acting like she has already won. But I swallow it down and say, "Your people at Pipe Creek stay there. Win or lose, they stay there until at least dawn."

She shrugs. "Fine. What else?"

"You agree to not go after the group that has already left," I say. "No chasing. No tracking them down. No games."

Her hazel eyes narrow and she stares at me taking a deep breath and letting out a long sigh. "As long as they never come back, and I get to add one more condition, that'll work."

"And your other condition?" I ask.

"After I beat you," she says with a twisted smile. "When you're lying senseless in the dust, there will be no interference from your people. I get to do with you what I will."

The thought of it twists my stomach, but then I realize that she doesn't mean to kill me here but to extend her game. And that works with what we have planned. "Agreed," I say.

"Well then," Talia says with a bright smile, pulling her T-shirt off. "Let's dance then, shall we?"

CHAPTER TWELVE

I BLAME it on the fever. The steroids have helped stabilize me, but my body is still fighting the infection and I have a fever.

It's a convenient excuse. Back when June and I were waiting for Talia and company, I told her I was going to ask her a question that I hoped would rattle Talia, but the question would be real.

I was going to ask her to marry me.

Now that we are in the corral and I'm stripping down to my tighty-blues—I'm not fond of white underwear—I realize what a colossally stupid idea it was and it must have been the fever.

Proposing to the woman of your dreams right before getting pummeled by your nemesis is definitely not a romantic idea. It certainly had a shot of rattling Talia, but doing it would forever stain the proposal.

This is what goes through my head as I kick off my boots and unbuckle my pants while Talia stares at me dressed only in her black underwear and a sports bra, a leering sneer on her face.

To stack on the terribleness of the idea, not only is Talia very likely to pummel me into oblivion, she is June's ex.

Even though it's a terrible idea, part of me wants to do it. It is an expression of love and I do love June and it just might be my last chance to express it.

Talia is covered in tattoos. From the snakes on her legs to the parts of wolves and tigers I can see on her belly, to the glimpses of a large dragon on her back.

She has decorated herself with predators because, I must assume, she views herself as a predator.

After the pants, I gingerly remove the half gloves. I've been wearing them for a while, the zombie scratches are weeping, and it hurts to take them off.

When I get a look at my hands, I'm surprised. They are red and weepy but the white thread isn't visible anymore. Maybe it's the steroids?

"That looks painful for you," Talia says with a saccharine sense of concern in her voice.

I ignore her and peel off the long-sleeved T-shirt, and "peel" is the right word. All those scratches have been weeping too and the shirt is painful to pull off my arms.

There are some gasps from Talia's people once they are all visible. There are dozens of them, they are deep and red and weeping, but they have closed up enough so no more white is visible.

"This is what happens when she doesn't like you," I say. "Or, rather, what happens when she doesn't like you and you are really lucky. Keep that in mind, boys."

During all this prelude to the fight, the rest of our people have slowly walked through the trees to the corral. Besides June, Dallas, Milo, Ralph, and Lisa, there are three other men and two other women, all armed, all with grim looks on their faces. I don't know any of them well, but June and Dallas do. They are the ones that chose to stay, that chose to fight Talia, making them my kind of people.

They are all hanging back behind Talia's people who are right at the edge of the corral. There are backward glances and glares but weapons stay holstered.

"Remember, everyone," Talia says loudly. "He is mine when this is all over."

And without anymore prelude, Talia attacks me.

I HAVEN'T BEEN in that many fights. A couple of times in high school, a couple of times after some contentious baseball games. I've landed some good hits and taken a few, but it wasn't ever a focus.

The one fight I really remember happened in junior high school. This guy named Roger, bigger and taller than me, took it on himself to tease me mercilessly about my freckles. I know, stupid, right?

During recess, he would lay into me until one day I took a swing at him. The freckle teasing, as it turns out, was just a pretext. I took the first swing, but he landed the first one and beat the crap out of me.

My father was very serious during the talk in the principal's office, but once we were outside of the school in the heat of a Phoenix spring, he said, "The key to winning a fight is not getting into a fight." But even with that said, he took me home and taught me a few things.

Not a lot, just some basics like watching your opponent's leading foot, watching their center of gravity, so you have a better idea what they are going to do.

When I got back to school, Roger kept teasing me about my freckles, but since I knew what the game was all about, I started teasing him about his skinny legs.

He didn't take kindly to it, and after only two recesses, he took a swing at me. It's not like I was suddenly a ninja or anything, but I did see it coming and stepped out of the way and he went sprawling onto the dirt and bloodied himself and got laughed at by most of the class.

All of this is to say that I am not a trained fighter, but I do know a few things. I do see Talia come charging in and take a swing at me and I sidestep her. She doesn't fall down but raises a cloud of dust with her abrupt stop and turns and faces me.

"This is gonna feel good," she says.

"Are you sure there is not any more cliched villainous things you want to say?" I ask as I back up. "Like, I don't know, 'No, Mr. Beckman, I expect you to die,' or 'This time it's personal.'"

"Shut up and bleed," she says.

"Yeah, like that," I say. "Very villainous. And it is really rather consistent with your lovely and winning personality."

She stops and stares at me, her eyes widening and looks around. "What's goin' on here?" she asks.

Hands go to their holsters as her people feed off her unease. Once Talia's people start reaching for their weapons, our people do too. Talia expected me to be scared and meek. I am certainly scared, but I'm honestly more scared of the fungus than I am of her right now.

The group mind is with me overlaying more sensations of the living. Their increasing heartbeats, the bundles of electricity concentrated in their heads and spines but sparking throughout their bodies.

I feel the two pods upstream on the Colorado start shambling into the water. As I explained, since I got lost in the Z-mind, it's been less of an argument and more of me being a node in the network. They know about the troops and Pipe Creek and that is where they are headed.

I also feel the group towards the North Rim near The Box start shambling out of the crevice they had crawled up down towards the trail.

"What did you expect?" June asks, breaking her silence and pulling me back to the present. "That we'd just lie down and let you take what you want?"

Talia turns her back to me and steps toward June. Guns aren't drawn yet, but everyone is tense, their hearts thumping away. This is a terrible position for us to be in. People in a circle start shooting at each other and there are going to be a lot of people going down.

"Somethin' like that," she says, her words hesitant as she continues to look around.

"You still think we don't know about your group marching down from the North Rim," June says. "We know everything, Talia, and we're ready for it all."

June and I didn't talk about this, we didn't plan for it, but if this continues, it will be a bloodbath and maybe part of June wants it. She wants the guns to come out. She wants this to be over.

Talia's swiveling head fixes on June, and without thinking about it, I charge. I dig my bare feet into the loose regolith like dirt and run as hard as I can. It's only ten feet or so, but I am a baseball player—or was—and sprinting is what I do.

A grunt escapes me as I set off and Talia must hear me because she turns around. It doesn't matter, though. By the time I reach her the grunt has turned into something of a growl and I plow into her, my shoulder hitting her in the gut and the air whooshes out of her.

We both go down hard with me on top of her and I think I hear one of her ribs crack.

What happens next is a bit of a blur to me. I think that charge started out as an attempt to stop a circular shootout, but by the time I connect with her it's become something else. I feel a rage in me for all the pain she has caused and the damage she has inflicted.

I'm hitting her as hard as I can with both fists. We're both on the ground, so it's not like there is much momentum to the blows, but it feels so good to have my fists connect with her flesh.

I'm dimly aware of shouts and cheers all around me, and a dimmer part of me is aware that the distraction is working, at least for now. I'm more aware of the galloping heartbeats around me and something so primitive coming from the Z-mind. I want to bite Talia's neck. I want to taste her blood. I've wanted nothing more in my entire life.

The lust and the hunger of all the Zs channel through me and there is nothing I can do to stop it. A zombie-like snarl escapes me as I open my mouth and lean in towards her neck.

Our eyes connect for a brief moment, and I see something unexpected. Fear. No, terror. She knows what is coming. She knows what I am becoming.

She jerks her knee up and connects it solidly with my groin. I am not snarling anymore but coughing and gasping. She pushes me off of her and gets to her feet.

"You know what," she says, spitting some blood out with the words. "It doesn't matter what you know. You all are goin' down."

And then she starts to kick me with her bare foot. But she knows what she is doing. She doesn't kick me like you would kick a soccer ball, she kicks me with the heel of her foot and I hear more ribs crack, and they are my own.

Instinctively, I pull into the fetal position and try to protect myself with my arms, but she grunts and kicks hard over and over. One of the kicks connects with my head and everything goes black.

CHAPTER THIRTEEN

THERE ARE voices shouting at me. Urgent voices that want me to get up.

I'm dimly aware of heat against my body, of movement, of something rough against the skin of my back side, of my left arm being stretched painfully as I am dragged over the ground.

But these aren't voices that are urging me and they aren't shouting. It's... I don't know what it is but it's more urgent than a voice and it's much closer.

They are desperate for me to open my eyes and get up. I'm clear it's a "they." This is not just one thing urging me, dragging me to consciousness, but many things.

I taste blood and a spiking pain is pulsing through my head. This is progress. I can taste and I have more of a sense of my body.

"Those were the terms," I hear a voice say, this time a real voice. "You all agreed to it. I get to do with him as I will."

There is a bit of a southern lilt to that voice, a quality I used to find quite delightful but now I hate. Talia.

"Not this," another voice says, and there is such pain in that voice that it drags me further towards consciousness.

"It's this or everyone starts shootin'," Talia says. "Which do you want, June-bug? Keep your word or let the bullets fly. Either is fine by me."

There is menace in her voice, to be sure, but something else. I've always thought of Talia as crazy, but a particular kind of crazy. This is different. She doesn't care if she lives or dies and that makes her very, very dangerous.

The voiceless urging redoubles. It's not words, but if it was, it would be something like, "Get up. Fight. We can help."

"Wait," I say, except I'm not fully functional yet and it comes out as "Whhaaa."

"What's that, Mr. Woodpecker?" Talia asks, and I feel her slap my cheek and none too gently. "Are ya back with us?"

"Wait," I say, this time the word is understandable. "Not. Done."

It sounds insane to me when it comes out, but it's all the non-voices urging me, the zombie group mind pouring itself into me. I realize that they don't want me to die, that they want me to stay part of their network, a meat brain with all the fungus brains. But it's more than that. They have a plan. And, I guess if I'm going to say that correctly, it should be "we" have a plan.

"You want more, Mr. Woodpecker?" Talia asks as I, with great effort, slit my eyes open. I can't quite focus, I'm seeing double, but still I make out Talia's angular face and her cruel eyes close to me. "You got more fight in ya?"

"Yes," I say. "But the name is Beckman."

She snorts. "Okay, *Beckman*. Let's see what ya got."

I try to move, but at first my body just won't respond, like the connections have been broken. For a moment I fear that one of Talia's kicks paralyzed me, but then it's like a switch is thrown and everything seems to work and I am moving.

A groan escapes me because it all hurts. I must have broken ribs because just breathing is a world of pain, but it's more than that. The pain in my head that spikes with every heartbeat, the constellation of pain in my gut, the scrapes along my back from being dragged wherever we are, I can barely move my left arm, and there is the deep pain of blossoming bruises on my arms and legs.

And then I hear the snarling and smell the rotting meat and fungus bouquet and I know we are down by the pen and I know what Talia is about to do to me. She is going to throw me in, make me one of her trophy Zs to be an object lesson to anyone who might think of challenging her.

Of course.

But Talia is out of date. This game is not just hers anymore. I chuckle, and using just my right arm, I push myself up into a sitting position, the world spinning around me.

"What the hell you laughin' at, Mr. Woodpecker?" Talia spits out.

"You've already lost," I say, trying to focus on her but still seeing double. "After you knocked me out, you gave a speech, didn't you? Declaring your victory and superiority. But you have already lost, you just don't know it yet."

Her forehead furrows and she looks around. She is still dressed in her underwear and I see the dark smudge of a blossoming bruise on her face and one on her shoulder. Maybe I was hitting her harder than I thought.

"What don't I know?" she asks.

I'm sucking in air trying to fight back the pain of the beating and the dragging, but I fear it's too much. I can't function like this. I can't stand.

But then I feel a flood of energy from the Z-mind. It's not energy, not really, it's more a clarity and an understanding about my body, about pain. And then it's like another switch is thrown, and while I am still in agony, it's no longer ruling me, no longer my world.

A distant part of me freaks out at this. This isn't a human switch that just got thrown, but a zombie switch. If they have any working nerves, they must all be in horrible pain all the time with how messed up their rotting forms are.

But that's just a distant part of me. I let out a sigh of relief. I'm still seeing two of everything, two of Talia, two each of her people. Two of June, a freaked out look on her beautiful faces. Two of Dallas, her faces twisted in pain as she stands close to Milo.

I ignore everyone but Talia. "Surrender, unconditionally," I say. "And I will guarantee your safe passage out of here."

She leans down and stares at me and then starts laughing. At first it's a chuckle and then it degrades into a psychotic cackle. I'm still focused on her, but out of my peripheral vision, I can see several of her men step back.

While she is cackling like the deranged maniac that she is, I stand up and pull my underwear back into place. They had slid down during the dragging and the back is full of holes, but it's the dignity I am afforded here, so I take it.

The zombie pen is behind me, the four of them snarling and reaching, and Talia is in front of me. I'm still seeing double, and now that I'm standing things start to spin.

I lean down bracing my hands on my thighs and squeeze my eyes shut so I can focus. "This is your only chance of survival," I say when her laughter dies down enough for her to hear me.

She starts laughing again. It's still a cackle but even less controlled, like a child caught in a laughter loop over the silliest thing. It's the laughter feeding the laughter now, not just what I said.

"He's right," June says. "There are more parties at play here than you know. That offer goes to all of you, surrender now and Woody will give you safe passage."

My eyes are closed, but I can feel hearts speed up, I can sense a slight change in the electrical patterns of their brains. I can't see with my eyes, but I know where everyone is.

"Yes," the Z-mind whispers to me. "This is the way. We are your eyes."

It's not words, just like the things I can sense are not seeing or feeling. It's a new sense, a different way of perceiving and under-standing, but the content of it is similar to those words.

I straighten up, my eyes still closed, bend my legs, and form a fist with my right hand. "Surrender or die," I say.

CHAPTER FOURTEEN

EXTINCTION OFTEN HAPPENS when the world changes and those living in that world can't adapt to the changes quickly enough.

The Zs coming was one such change for humanity—we are nearly extinct. The Zs growing a group mind is a further compounding of that. Any of the living out there that don't recognize this change fast enough, even the ones that did well surviving before the pods formed, will be gone, and soon.

On a small level, the same thing has happened to Talia and company. They believe they understand the way the world works, that they know how to thrive in this world, how to rule, how to violently bend it to their will, but the rules have changed. Dramatically.

As I stand there with my eyes closed sensing those around me, living and dead, this is abundantly clear to me. I just hope that I am in touch enough with the new rules, that I can adapt fast enough.

My body is screaming in pain but the Zs have shown me how to ignore it. Not that I can ignore its limits—my left arm is numb and fairly useless and, except for my underwear, I am naked. I'm injured, bruised, and scraped standing under the blue Arizona sky at the bottom of the Grand Canyon facing someone far more capable and in much better shape.

I guess it would be reasonable for Talia to not recognize that things have changed, to not believe me. And, frankly, if it was just me, I wouldn't have been doing what I was doing. It is the collective confidence of the Z-mind that lets me stand there with my eyes closed beaten to shit challenging a trained warrior who just kicked my ass to fight some more.

It's an oddly peaceful moment. I'm not fighting the group mind anymore. I'm not fighting the pain or my body's limitations. I just am. I have enough awareness to know that survival is far from assured, that whatever the future holds for me, it won't be a perfect Zen moment like this one, but I relax into it and do my best to let the experience sink into me.

"I'll never surrender," Talia hisses. "And it's your turn to die."

I smile. I want to throw a sharp rejoinder back at her, something along the lines of what a perfectly cliched villain she is acting like, but I am too deep for that.

I sense her moving. I feel a rush of air. Those witnessing are suddenly silent. I move to the left, but her foot catches me in the chest and sends me stumbling back over the rocky land and banging into the zombie pen.

Rough hands reach for me, grab me, and the fetid stench of them briefly makes me want to retch, but I can switch that off too. The Zs are hungry, starving. No, "we" are hungry, starving. My heart is beating and that makes me food.

There is a brief dissonance in my mind, the hall of mirror effect I've described before as the four Zs sense edible human flesh, as I sense them, as we sense each other, as the Z-mind decides what *we* are doing.

With a pronounced snarl, the Zs let me go and I feel several scratches on my shoulders and back as a grasping hands with ripped nails withdraw and then the snarling stops. I sense them move back from me, using the pen to stay standing despite their broken legs, and then they are quiet.

There are gasps and Talia says, "What the..."

I step forward, my eyes still squeezed shut, and swivel my head and "look" right at Talia. "I will say this one more time. Surrender now or die."

Some of Talia's people take another step back. Dallas swears and there are low murmurs.

The sun has set and it's starting to get dark. I can feel the Zs floating down the Colorado River and the group at The Box has hit the trail and they are all lying down, playing dead.

I almost gasp when I sense it.

Back up on Tanner Trail with the group there that attacked June and then me, part of them pretended to be the old-style, dumb as a pound of nails Zs while the others closed in from behind silently. They were playing into our expectations of how Zs act strategically to make a meal of us. But this, playing dead up at The Box, this is a whole new level and I know they got this from me, when I was locked in the Z-mind under the cottonwood tree. They learned this from me and now every other Z that gets in range will know it too.

The Zs just got smarter and I helped them.

"I don't know what the hell kinda game this is," Talia says, the laughter gone and her voice menacing. "But I will never surrender."

She doesn't hesitate any longer or deliver anymore villainous lines but rushes me without warning. I shouldn't see it coming, but I do. This is not some sophisticated attack but a freight-train like rush, the kind of thing I just did to her in the corral.

I awkwardly leap out of the way and she goes stumbling into the zombie pen, crashing into the wood with a curse, her arms and head extending over the low wall. One of my feet lands on a loose rock and I fall and hit the ground hard.

I feel a sensation that I will never forget and I fear will haunt my dreams. It's a sense of joy so pure, so light, so high that I let out another gasp. It's the high of knowing the thing you want most has just been delivered to you and everything is going to be all right.

The feeling is coming from the Harris Z and the other three in the pen. They don't hesitate. They move with unusual speed for Zs, especially considering their broken legs, and are on Talia before she can recover. They grab her while she is opening up her mouth to spit out another curse.

My eyes fly open and I see the Harris Z sink his teeth into the bare flesh of Talia's shoulder. I feel the joy the Z is feeling at the same time. It feels like it's my teeth sinking into Talia, and in some bizarre way it is.

I'm still kind of seeing double, but it's getting better. There is another Z biting on her other shoulder as the other two bite into her arms.

Talia screams and I feel the Zs' triumphant joy as counterpoint. They all four take their chunk of flesh, the wounds bleeding profusely as their mangled hands drag her roughly over the wall into the pen.

I look away. I can sense it all but I can't watch it too. June is looking away, a pinched look on her face. Dallas is looking down. The blond man who seems to be Talia's second has his gun drawn and pointing at the Zs, and several others do too, but none of them fire. Because it's too late for Talia.

I get up and stumble forward and look him in the eye and say, "Leave. Now. You will not have a second chance."

And yeah, I'm beat to shit, dizzy, and barely standing there dressed in only my ripped underwear, but my words are accompanied by Talia's screams, and after all they just witnessed it doesn't take long. They share a few looks and then they hustle off down the path towards the bridge and the rest of Talia's men at Pipe Creek.

After they're gone, I stand there swaying. Talia's screams have stopped and the Zs are hanging on to the pen walls staring at her now still form. They didn't eat that much of her, just a bite or two each and then they turned their backs on their insatiable hunger and they stopped.

I feel Talia's heart stop beating and a wave of sorrow crashes over me. She is dead, but not gone. She'll be a Z soon trapped in the pen she made with the other Zs she created.

Justice? Perhaps, but it's still a bitter pill.

"I..." I begin and everyone looks at me. Their faces vary from curious to terrified, to exhausted, to completely freaked out. A combination of them all, really. The world spins and I sway on my feet. "I think I need to lie down," I say.

And then I do, right there on the dirt in front of the zombie pen. Well... I don't "lie" down. I fall down and I know nothing for a very long time.

CHAPTER FIFTEEN

WHILE I'M UNCONSCIOUS, my dreams are not dreams. At least not at first. I'm still fully part of the Z-mind as they feast, as they apply strategies cooked up, in part, by my meat-mind.

The Zs floating down the river "wash" up on the shore of Pipe Creek, their bodies floating face down. First a few float up the beach and then the calm waters next to it are thick with them.

The two men guarding the beach are on edge already. I can feel their nervousness, their fluttering hearts. They must have been told what happened to Talia.

The rest of Talia's men are clumped together just up the trail in the stone rest house that was designed to shield hikers from the brutal heat of this part of the hike. I'm sure they are talking, planning, deciding how to take Phantom Ranch. How to exact revenge for their fallen leader.

The two men on the beach approach the floating bodies slowly, carefully, but the Zs don't move. They seem harmless, they might even guess that Zs can drown because their heads are intact.

Whatever they are thinking, they don't expect the hands that grab them, that pull them down into the water, that silence them with hungry mouths before they can alert the rest of the men.

It goes on from there with the zombies surrounding the men in the rest house in silence and attacking only when their victory is assured. It's not a pleasant dream full of screams, mixed with the utter joy of the Zs feasting.

A few of them get away, a small band of five men, three that managed to escape the rest house and two others that had been guarding the trail farther up. There is gunfire, some Zs fall, but it's dark, and the men were surprised. Most of their bullets miss their mark, hitting a Z in the arm or the chest or somewhere else that doesn't count.

And then the zombie tourist horde finally dines and in my dreams I am witness to it all, I am part of it all. Quite a few of them are treated like Talia and only bitten a few times so they can add to their numbers.

The scene at The Box is much the same, but the Zs there outnumber the living hiking down. Maybe Talia's men in their freak out, and then in their demise forgot to radio them an update. Maybe the nature of The Box made it so the walkie-talkies didn't work, but that group comes to a narrow area of the canyon filled with inert bodies.

It's dark. They have orders. They try to rush through and the mostly-dead come alive and pull them down and feast. None escape.

The feasting part of the dream goes on and on, it's like I can't escape it, like it will never stop. But it does. Finally. And the Zs leave.

I feel the Z-mind evaluate their needs, their energy, their goals. I am part of that calculus. In fact, my unconscious mind is actively participating, actively advocating for my continued existence and the living at Phantom Ranch. Claiming this area as mine.

It takes a long time for the Z-mind to settle, but in the end the two groups shamble away back up the trails to find other meals, leaving only the four Zs in the pen and a few stragglers here and there to keep the Z-mind alive across the canyon.

The battle is won, but even in my dreaming state, I fear that my humanity is lost.

The dreams still haunt me, a mix of my revulsion of what happened and the joy of the starving Zs that finally get to eat. I feel relief that our immediate threat is gone and fear of the future when the Zs are done with me and decide that Phantom Ranch is where their next meal will come from.

CHAPTER SIXTEEN

"HEY," a voice says, distant and gentle, a female voice. "Are you with me, Woody?"

The dream that wasn't a dream echoes in my mind and I want to escape it, but I am so tired. And in so much pain. It hurts to breathe and it feels like I just came out of a giant dryer where I had been tossed around for a few days. There are hot lines of pain on my shoulders and back where the zombies just scratched me.

"Tell him we're in the clear," another voice says, another female. "That his army of the undead triumphed and then left. Tell him the queen bitch of the desert is in the pen she created snarling like the animal she is."

"I think he knows that," the first voice says.

"Tell him Sal and Mary dragged their asses back to camp shortly after Talia got her due, handcuffed together and singing his praises," the second voice says.

"That's not important," the first one says.

"Was he doing that snapping jaw thing again?" the second voice asks.

"Yeah," the first one says.

A dim part of me knows that the first voice is June and the second is Dallas, but it's not enough for me to surface, not yet. I am drawn back down into the dream that is now a memory, down into the feast of flesh.

"COME ON, WOODY," the first voice says the next time consciousness and pain start to return. "You've got to fight this. Please. You were going to ask me a question before the fight with Talia, but you never did. I really wanted you to ask me that question."

I feel her take my hand and squeeze. Her hand feels cool to me, cold really, and I am dimly aware that it's not just injuries that I'm fighting but that the fever is back and I am fighting the fungus.

I shift my body, trying to move, my backside is numb from being in the same position too long, but I am strapped down and can't move much at all.

"Please," June says again. "Fight, Woody, fight."

"Are the whites of his eyes yellow?" the second voice asks. It's Dallas.

"Just... just a little," June says.

"The cuts are healing, though, right?" Dallas asks. "Even the new ones on his shoulders and back. You can't see the white anymore, right?"

"No," June says, "But..." I feel gentle pressure at my forearms. "His body is different than it was. When he first told me down by the Colorado about the white in the scratches, I wasn't sure, but now I am. I think the new scratches reactivated the infection somehow, made it worse."

"Fungus," Dallas says and the word is harsh and full of fear.

June sighs. "Yes. I think it's deeper now."

"We're going to have to try it, aren't we?" Dallas asks.

"Yes," June says with defeat and resignation in her voice.

"And it could kill him, right?" Dallas asks.

"This much steroid injected into his bloodstream," June says.

"Yeah, it could kill him. It should kill him. But the pills aren't working and smaller doses aren't either."

"We have to try," Dallas says.

"I know," June says. "There's an anti-fungal in here too. All we've got. If this doesn't work..."

"Just do it," Dallas says.

I feel a prick at my arm and I try to speak, but I don't have the energy and the dreams pulls me back down.

"I DON'T WANT to have to leave you, Woody," June says as consciousness returns. "But I made a promise."

This time the pain is there but it's more bearable—just normal pain. It hurts to breathe still but not so much and I am sore all over and weak as a kitten.

I hear the whispers of the zombie group mind, sensory information flowing in, but it's disjointed and vague. I get the sense of Zs assembled at the South Rim and the North Rim, a small group of Zs close by, and a few spread in between to form the mesh network, but that is about it. I feel their interest in me, but it all seems like a low bandwidth connection now instead of being plugged directly into like I was when I was fighting Talia.

I can sense the other two presences in the room and some outside too, but it's more like a simple radar and there's not much more information to it than that. It's almost like when I first saw the fungus deep in my scratches.

"Wade's family is still in Flagstaff," June says. "I promised him we would rescue them, but... Listen, Woody, the Zs left but only went as far as the rims. I think it's still about you. We really need you, but I made a promise and I can't wait much longer."

After all our fanciful theorizing about the origin of the zombie apocalypse (i.e. aliens, time travel, a sentient planet) I am beginning to fear it really is just evolution. The fungus evolved so it could use humans as a host. And maybe what is happening to me is part of that same evolution.

"You... you should be better now," June says, taking my hand and squeezing it. "The treatments worked and they didn't kill you. I think the fungus is still there, but now your body is winning. You should be waking up now but you are not. I don't understand why."

I try to say something, but only a groan escapes my mouth. I move and find that I am not tied down anymore and that makes what June just said seem real.

The dreams are still there, the dreams of flesh consumed and the joy of it and I am terrified of being drawn back down into them. I try to speak again, but it comes out as a groan, one that sounds rather zombie-like. Not quite a snarl but close enough to scare me.

June lets go of my hand. It must have scared her too. "Woody..." she says. "Please, Woody. Please." Her voice is so full of sorrow that I can't stand it.

I take a deep breath and focus all my energy on speaking one word. The same word I spoke to Talia to keep her from throwing me in the zombie pen. "Wait," I say, and this time it is intelligible but very quiet.

"What?" June asks, holding my hand again and I can feel her leaning close. "What did you say?"

"Wait," I say again, this time a little louder. "Wait. For. Me."

June laughs, it's all high-pitched tension release, but it is laughter nonetheless which makes my three goals for the day seem assured. I'm with June and she laughed, that's number three and number two respectively, and survival, number one, seems pretty much a lock and that makes this a very good day.

I feel her cheek against mine and it's wet with tears and then she kisses me on the cheek.

"Lips," I say and she laughs some more and kisses me on the lips. I'm not all there yet, so it's not exactly a passionate kiss, but it's my June and what else could I ask for?

I slit my eyes open and I have trouble focusing, but the first thing

I see are June's ocean-blue eyes framed in her beautiful face. It's all a bit blurry, I can tell I'm in one of the cabins, but I can see that she's got dark circles under those eyes and her face looks drawn. "You look like shit," I say, happy that I can get a full sentence out.

"I look the picture of health compared to you," she says.

I nod and even that is hard. "Sleepy," I say. "But wait for me, okay? Let's rescue Wade's family. Together."

She smiles and I can't help but smile back. "Together," she says, and then adds the Spanish word for always. "*Siempre.*"

"In the meantime, get in this bed, June," I say. Her brow furrows and quirky smile plays on her lips. "Not that," I add. "We both need a nap."

She nods and lies down next to and holds me tight as I finally sleep peacefully and don't get sucked back down into the zombie feeding nightmare.

CHAPTER SEVENTEEN

"HEY, DIAMONDBACK," Dallas says gently the next time I wake up. She's sitting on the side of my bed and June is gone. I feel much more awake and my eyes can focus enough for me to look around. I'm in one of the historic cabins in a queen bed. The room is simple with dark wood paneling on the walls, a stone fireplace in one corner, a sink in another corner, and windows which are made up of small panes.

"Hey, Lonestar," I say.

"Glad you're not a Z," she says, a smile lighting up her face. She looks like she's gained a little weight, her face a little fuller than I remember, more like when we first met. It's all marred a bit from the fresh bruise around her right eye, but I'm still glad to see her looking well.

"Me too," I say. "How long?"

"How long since you and your minions saved our asses?" she asks.

The use of the term "minions" is extremely uncomfortable, but I just swallow it down and nod.

"Six days," she says. "I've got some broth here. June really wants you to drink it."

"Can I get some coffee instead?" I ask.

She gives me a half smile and says, "None to be found down here, but I spiked it will a little green tea when June wasn't looking."

I stare at her for a moment. Green tea is not what one imagines Dallas spiking something with and broth and green tea sounds kinda bad, but at this point being able to consume any calories is a victory. "Any caffeine in an apocalypse," I say, trying to smile but I figure it looks more like a grimace.

"Can you sit up?" she asks.

I nod and try to push myself up in the bed but find I don't have the strength. I groan and say, "I need help."

Dallas nods but keeps any comments to herself and helps me get into a sitting position. I am weak, so weak, but I'm not dizzy and I don't feel like I have a fever, so that's a definite win.

But then it hits me and I feel my heart reluctantly start thumping in my chest. "Is... is June still here?"

Dallas bites her lip. "Yeah. Wade is losing it, but Milo and Lisa hiked up far enough to get some drone footage of the South Rim Village and it's zombie city. No one's going anywhere without you."

She holds a cup for me with a straw in it and I take a sip. It's lukewarm, salty, a little earthy from the tea, and it tastes pretty much like the best meal I've ever had at this point, but I go slow.

After a few more sips I find that she's staring at me, her frown lines earning their keep, a look of deep concern on her face.

"What?" I ask. "Do I look that bad?"

She smiles, but the frown quickly returns. "You look like shit," she says. "That's for sure. But, no, there's just... something we need to talk about."

"What!?" I ask, feeling my heart sputter to life and try to speed to a gallop, but instead it just clomps along awkwardly for a few beats before returning to normal.

"When I was the bomb," she begins, her fingers playing with the sheet on the bed, her eyes anywhere but looking at me. "When you were saving me. I... I said some shit."

My heart does a better job of speeding up as I remember the

"throuple" hints that Dallas laid on me when I was trying to save her life down here in that small corral, when she had the murder vest on.

"You said a lot of things," I say, smiling. It's the same thing I said to her then when she started the conversation in the corral, but I think that is lost on her. Dallas is fierce but this seems to scare her.

"You know what I'm talking about," she says, her brown eyes briefly meeting mine before darting away.

Pre-apocalypse, hell, even pre-zombie fungal infection, I would have avoided this kind of conversation like... well, like a zombie fungal infection. But now? Bring it on. These are words and emotions, and yeah, they can get totally fraught, but Dallas is family. I love her. I owe her me being the best version of myself as much as I can manage. Even if I'm just newly conscious from my second round of almost dying from that zombie fungal infection.

"I do," I say smiling. I reach out and touch her chin gently so that she is looking at me. "What I said after the raft bucked us out and we had to swim the Colorado is still true."

"You said a lot of shit," she says, smiling a little at throwing that line back at me.

"I know you better now," I say. "And I love you even more. You are, seriously, the whole package, but... June. My heart wants June."

Dallas's face lights up and those frown lines turn into smile lines. Her eyes widen and she does a little miniature fist pump.

"What?" I ask. "What did I miss?"

She shakes her head. "Oh, nothing. A girl just needs to hear that sometimes. I just wanted to tell you that I have other prospects now and you don't have to break your poor little male ego trying to be enough for both June and me."

My jaw opens as my cheeks flush hot, but I just can't find the words. Sure, Dallas has made it a habit of teasing me, and I just wrote all that stuff about being up for anything because I am still alive, but this feels like a little too much.

She gets up and walks to the door of the room. "Drink that broth now."

Dallas has a pronounced limp, but I am happy to see that she is walking, that her ankle is getting better. I almost say something but then it hits me and I say, "It's Milo, isn't it?"

She takes a step back towards me. "Do you think...?"

Dallas doubts herself, despite her beautiful, curvy appeal and fascinating personality. She doubts that she can find someone in all of this mess.

Hell, I can't blame her. It was always a crapshoot, and I didn't do very well pre-apocalypse.

"Yes," I say. "I saw how he looked at you when Talia was getting ready to pummel me."

She cocks her head and her brow furrows. "Really?"

I nod and sigh. "And I could sense something." She's still staring at me so I add, "Believe me, when you are about to get your ass kicked, you'll focus on any little thing."

She slowly shakes her head. "You do love me, Woody."

"Well... yeah," I say. "Haven't I said it enough times by now?"

She takes another step forward, her stare intense. "But one more thing," she says. "And I have discussed this with June."

"What...?" I say, pretty sure despite my earlier statements that I am not ready for this, whatever it is.

"I reserve the right to have a child and..." She trails off, her eyes wandering around the room landing on the stone fireplace. I mean, it's lovely, but she's looking at it like it's the most fascinating thing in the world.

"Okay...?" I say, wondering what this is about.

Dallas sighs and walks back over and sits on the bed, her eyes wandering for a while before they meet mine. "You know that bull-shit about women and their 'biological' clock?"

I shrug. "Yeah..." I mean, I've heard such things, but given my gender I don't feel qualified to comment.

"It's not all bullshit," she says. "I've been feeling..." She gets up and paces around the room. "Maybe it's what's going on. God knows

I didn't feel this way before the Zs, but lately..." She trails off and stares at me.

"You're feeling like you want to bring life into a world where so much has been lost," I offer.

She nods and I swear she tears up a little. "It's insane. Completely insane. But if things get stable here... you know..."

"Preservation of the human race, right?" I say.

She nods.

This whole discussion makes me think of June and I wonder if she is thinking the same thing and the thought just freaks me the hell out.

It must have shown on my face because Dallas comes back and sits down on the bed and says, "Don't worry. June's uterus isn't open for business. I'm sure you all will get around to talking about it at some point."

I open my mouth but I have absolutely nothing to say. Hell, I don't even know what I think about it.

"And that brings us back to *my* uterus," Dallas says with a twisted little smile.

I have no idea what she is getting at. "What's going on, Dallas?" I ask.

She takes a deep breath, sits up straight, and says, "As your best friend. As the social lubricant that aided you and June becoming what you are, I..." She looks away again.

"Just say it, Dallas. Please," I say.

She looks back at me and her face is fierce. "As your best friend, I reserve the right to have *your* baby."

My jaw flops open again. I have no words and fear I will never have any words ever again.

Dallas stares at me like she expects me to be able to speak, and when I don't, she says, "Look at it this way, if we are going to restart humanity, we're going to have to mix the genes up. The old rules are out."

My jaw is still hanging open.

"And," she says with a shrug, "I want my kid to have those fungus-resistant genes of yours. You should be dead, Woody. Several times over."

I still can't speak.

Her face darkens and she turns away. "And... and you're my best friend," she says. "Please. Just say something."

I want to make a joke, tease her about her biological clock, but Dallas doesn't make herself vulnerable often or easily.

"We're talking turkey baster here?" I ask when I can finally speak.

Her face scrunches up and she looks insulted. "God, no. I will not have life created inside of me with a cheap piece of plastic. We are talking the normal way."

"And... June is okay with this?" I ask.

She nods. "If it's... what did she say? If it's 'for the expressed purpose of knocking me up' she's fine with it."

My jaw dangles some more. "I... I don't understand women."

Dallas's face lights up. "But aren't we fabulous?"

I nod but don't say anything else.

"Well..." Dallas asks, poking me in the side which happens to be near a broken rib so I yelp in pain.

"What about Milo?" I ask.

She rolls her eyes. "That's theoretical so far and my problem, not yours. So what do you say, Woody?"

So I get that this is some kind of cliched male fantasy. I get that the biological imperative for a male is to "spread the seed." And I get that Dallas is an attractive woman.

But I also get that this is the apocalypse and bringing a child into it is more than a little complicated, that human emotions are tricky things, and that I am wired for monogamy. I also get that this is something Dallas really wants.

"Down the line a little bit?" I ask.

She nods and smiles.

"With June's blessing?"

She nods and smiles wider. "She can be part of the proceedings, if you like."

I can't speak, yet again.

"You're doing that blinky thing, Woody," she says, with a laugh. "And it is adorable. I take this as a sign that you are on the road to recovery."

I shrug and say, "Who am I to say no to my best friend."

She hugs me hard and I think she cracks another rib.

I really don't understand women.

It takes me a while to get back to sleep, but when I do I have a different kind of dream, not zombie feasts or impregnating best friends. One that's not quite a dream, one I need to do something about.

CHAPTER EIGHTEEN

"ARE you really okay with this Dallas thing?" I ask June. I'm leaning on her as we walk down a dusty trail in Phantom Ranch.

It's pretty early, the sun's not up above the canyon yet, and it hasn't gotten hot. There is a gathering crowd of people staring at us but keeping their distance for the most part.

"Sure," she says. "Limited use only. You're all mine."

I think I should correct that. They are not staring at "us", they are staring at me. Not everyone was here for the fight with Talia, but everyone knows what happened and I expect the tale has grown in the telling.

"It seems risky to me," I say.

"Why?" June asks, and there is something playful in her voice.

We are slowly passing the corral, the one where Dallas was the bomb and we dangled over it for a few hours while June got control of Phantom Ranch. I give it the side-eye as we slowly walk by.

"Humans are complicated," I say. "Emotions can be fraught."

I feel June shrug under my arm. "This thing goes too far and... well, let's just say I'll make sure it doesn't go too far."

I stop and disengage so I can see her ocean-blue eyes. "This doesn't worry you?"

She smiles and it's genuine. June seems different, more relaxed, happier. "Could this turn into a huge mess?" she asks. "Sure. But it's all love with the three of us, right?"

I nod.

"We'll work it out," she says. She pauses and then adds, "Remember that this is your genetic material we are talking about. This is you becoming a father. You have some say in how this goes down."

I know I'm blinking too much again and I'm grateful June doesn't say anything about it, but there is a smile playing on her lips. "So... turkey baster," I say.

"Dallas will fight it," June says, her shoulders shrugging under my arm again. "She wants what she wants. The question is, how badly she wants your genes."

As we walk down the dusty trail, I can see that June is right. Dallas will be very noisy but ultimately she will compromise. I can also see that Dallas chose to spring this on me when I was quite weak and that her rejection of the turkey baster idea may not be quite as real as she made it out to be. She will be forever teasing me and I will be forever grateful for it.

"Although..." June begins, clear signs of amusement in her voice now. "Dallas is damn sexy. Not sure why you'd want to turn that down."

"I swear I don't understand women," I say.

June chuckles. "I don't sometimes, myself. And besides, on the Zs trying to eat us and Talia torturing us with her psychotic game scale, this ain't no big deal."

We lapse into silence as I concentrate on ambulation and try not to think about all the stares or about fatherhood.

Back in the early days of this when we found out Dallas was working for Talia, when June knocked Dallas out instead of killing her, she said, "We're not like them." It's this moment in my mind where I knew I was all in with June. She had managed, somehow, to retain her humanity in the apocalypse and that is no small thing.

But now, I am literally not like them. I am something different, and all the stares make me feel like this is another moment like that, somehow.

June is here with me, and Dallas wants me to father her child, so I am clearly not alone, but I just don't know what me being "not like them" means for our future.

And with what is about to happen, the whole of Phantom Ranch is going to become aware of just how not like them I now am.

I smell them before I see them, the rotting, moldy bouquet of the penned Zs floating up the trail on the morning breeze. The roof of the old ranger station is visible with the cliffs beyond, a mesquite tree and a cottonwood hanging over the trail, and a huge bunch of prickly pear cactus just off it.

"You sure about this?" June asks.

I told her about the new dream that's not a dream and what I need to do. "Yeah," I say. "They're not quite what we thought they were."

When I can see the zombie pen, I can also see the crowd that has already gathered. The faces are hard and wary and I don't blame them. Not one bit. But they are not like I am—they don't know what these Zs are experiencing.

She shakes her head. "But they still want to eat us," she says.

"Yes," I say. "So why didn't someone put a bullet in their heads while I was out?"

"Some wanted to," she says. "But the Zs left after they took care of Talia's people. We all know that is about you, Woody."

We are silent for a little bit as we make our slow way. It's not lost on me that the speed I am capable of is very zombie-like. That I lost a lot of weight fighting this infection and I still look like hell. Not quite as bad as a Z, but I don't quite look human yet. And I sure don't feel human yet.

"You're going to have to give a speech," she says.

I groan but then stifle it. I don't want to sound like a Z too.

"Yeah," I say. "I bet I do."

HOW DO I describe this scene so it makes sense? So you understand?

I guess we should start with the Zs. There are five of them in the pen Talia built out of old two-by-fours, about four feet tall with a gate on the downhill side. On that gate is a sign made out of old plywood and thick red paint that reads "Mess with them and you are next."

The irony here is that the fifth Z is Talia. She looks pretty much the same, still in her underwear, still covered in her predator tattoos, but she's dirty with several hunks of flesh gone from her shoulders and arms, her eyes zombie yellow as she hisses and reaches for me.

I'm standing at the south end of the pen near the gate that was built into it. I'm standing on my own, which isn't easy. I'm not dizzy, and I'm so grateful for that, but I am still so weak and very sore.

Zombie Talia can't reach me because a couple of ropes were tossed over her and she is being held by Milo and Ralph from the other side of the pen. This doesn't keep her from snarling and reaching for me, specifically. And I'm sure it's me because I can feel her anger through the zombie group mind.

The other four Zs, Harris, Al, Fiona, and Henry are away from the Talia Z, holding themselves up on the sides of the pen, their yellow eyes more or less staring at me.

It's an odd scene, even for the apocalypse.

June is standing with Dallas a few feet away from me and around us are most of the residents of Phantom Ranch. Their faces are hard, many arms crossed, close to twenty people in all. There are no children, but beyond that the age variance is pretty wide, but the one thing they have in common is the hard look of survivors. Rough clothing. Sunburned skin. Lean bodies. Wary eyes.

"I know you all don't really know me," I say, my voice a little rough so I clear my throat. "I know what I am must be confusing to you. It sure is to me. But let me try to explain it so you understand what I want to do."

I pause looking around. There are some friendlier faces out there. Meryl gives me a small smile and nod, wearing his Grateful Dead T-shirt, of course. Lisa is standing next to him and I see compassion in her brown eyes. I'm sure June and Dallas have filled her in on a lot of the details. Sal and Mary are there, both of them giving me an appraising look that I think represents the middle ground of opinions.

My mouth goes dry and I can't find the words. I'm not a speech kind of a guy in the first place, but how do I talk about this?

"I want to let these four Zs go," I say. "Not Talia, of course, but the other four." People shift, some backwards, and more arms are crossed. "I get how that sounds crazy, but they don't want to be here. They want to return—they want to be with other Zs. I can feel it in my dreams. They..."

I trail off. This is impossible. This makes so little sense to me, how can I make anyone else understand?

But then it occurs to me that I have been talking about this, or "writing" about this all along. I've been spending much of my recovery time catching these diaries up. This is a story and I know how to tell stories. Maybe it doesn't make sense to go back all the way, but I do.

I take a deep breath and say, "To understand this, I need to tell you a story, one I am calling 'Woody and June versus the Apocalypse.' It all began not that long ago on a cold spring morning at a dog food plant in Flagstaff, Arizona..."

CHAPTER NINETEEN

I DON'T TELL them the whole story, not in the detail I am telling it here, that would have taken days. But I take them step by step through the forty days between when I met June and when Talia ended up in that pen.

I explain the zombie group mind and how I became a part of it as honestly and openly as I can. I tell them how when I first got down here, I could feel Harris in particular and his anger at Talia at what she had done, how the Zs still retain some of what they were, how Harris's anger at Talia and his influence on the zombie group mind put Phantom Ranch at risk.

I tell them of the truce that we seem to be in with the Zs that are now mostly up on the rim. How it is important to honor that truce by not killing or harming the Zs if we don't have to.

And I tell them about how in my dreams, I now feel Harris again and his need to be free of this place, how important it is to him.

And, yes, I'm thinking of the Harris zombie as a "him" not an "it" now. The Zs are not human and they will eat us if they get the chance, but given the rather brutal food chain of biology it kind of makes sense. Humanity now has a predator... besides itself, that is.

And I guess you could consider the Zs as humanity still preying on itself, but I don't see it that way. The Zs used to be us but now they are something different.

There is a debate and a vote. I don't feel the need to detail that here. That is part of the life that I hope I get to lead, the politics of living with a group of people and that's not what these diaries are about.

In the end, the majority of Phantom Ranch survivors agree, the word goes out to not interfere with them, and I open the gate and step back.

It's a weird moment, almost indescribable. The living are quiet and so are the dead except for the Talia zombie who is hissing and reaching for me but can't move because of the ropes Milo and Ralph have around her.

The Zs stay there for a moment, still looking dumbly in the direction I had been before I opened the gate, each clinging to the wall of the pen because of their broken legs. It's only a few seconds, but it feels much longer, and then the Harris Z awkwardly hops to the gate, using the pen to support himself until he is at the opening, freedom in front of him. He turns his head until he is looking right at me.

I feel him through the group mind, I see him with my eyes, and I sense him looking at me. I'm not so connected to the group mind so that it is a hall of mirrors, but it's a strange little echo.

There are a few low voices in the crowd. Some are probably wondering if I'm about to be their next meal. Hell, some are probably hoping for it. I am an anomaly and societies are often unkind to anomalies.

The moment doesn't last long before the Harris Z takes a step forward, stumbles out of the pen, and promptly falls to the ground, his broken legs unable to support him.

He pushes himself up on his hands, clearly ready to drag his broken body away from here, but he stops and stares at me, and his eyes—I kid you not—remind me of a hurt puppy that doesn't know what's wrong with them.

I know what he wants. I can feel it. But this is a lot. This is too much. I'm going to lose these people. They are going to turn on me.

But this is my path. It doesn't matter one bit to me in that moment if it's harder than I thought, if it doesn't end well. I made the choice.

"Strong, straight branches," I say. "Or some two-by-fours about eighteen inches long. I need them. And rope."

June is staring at me, blinking too fast. I'm looking at her when I add, "Please."

She licks her lips, her smooth brow furrows, and I can see her thinking it over, weighing her trust of me against the insane thing I am clearly asking for.

This is it. This is the moment where our relationship bends and shows its strength or snaps and breaks.

Does she trust me? Does she trust my judgment? And, more importantly, should she? I am infected. If the fungus has changed me isn't the question, it's how much, and here I am wanting to do first aid on zombies.

It's a long few seconds, but it's only a few seconds. "Meryl, Wade," she says looking at the two men. "Help me. Now."

As they run off, I turn and face the survivors living here at Phantom Ranch. "This must seem crazy to you," I say, my mouth dry and my words feeling a little strange.

There are a few nods and a few of them look away, but I lock eyes with Dallas who gives me a smile, a small one holding a whole lot of crazy, and a nod.

I take a deep breath and feel the instinct I had been operating on becoming clear enough to express. "Honestly, it seems a little crazy to me too," I say, "but these Zs aren't fighting us. They want to leave. They want to be with others of their kind."

The other three Zs are still in the pen supporting themselves on the walls, not trying to leave, while the Harris zombie is on the dusty ground just outside the pen and just off the trail. He's staring at me, his need echoing in my mind. To illustrate what I just said, I take a step back and continue to stare at my fellow survivors. I am close enough for Harris Z to attack me, I am facing away from him. I let my actions speak louder than my words.

"Peace," I say, when it's clear he's not going to attack me, that I'm not going to be his victim, that the Zs aren't quite what we thought they were. "We have to take peace whenever and wherever we can find it. Especially now."

IT'S ANOTHER STANDOFF. Me close enough for the Harris zombie to bite while I face off against the crowd. The dank smell of rotting flesh fills my nose and my stomach is turning. I'm sweating, and not just from the relentless Arizona sun. The Phantom Ranch survivors could turn on me just as easily as the Zs. They could attack us all, but they don't.

Maybe it's my message of peace, but, honestly, it seems like it's more about the strangeness of the scene with me being close enough for the Harris Z to attack.

Or maybe I'm not giving them enough credit. Harris used to be one of them. All of these Zs did. Maybe we are all sick of killing Zs that used to be people we knew. People we cared about. People we loved.

It only lasts a few minutes, but it feels like another eternity of time, the sun beating down on us, the cool gurgle of Bright Angel Creek, the sounds of birds, and feet shuffling on the dry ground all that is filling the silence.

We are all stuck, it would seem, between fear and fear. Fear of doing what I am suggesting, aiding zombies, letting them go. And fear of not doing what I am suggesting and killing the only peaceful Zs any of us have ever seen.

We are not stuck for long. June jogs back ahead of Meryl and Wade with an arm full of sticks and ropes. Her blue eyes go wide when she sees how close to the Harris Z I am, but she makes no comment. She dumps the supplies in front of me and asks, "Now what?"

I clear my throat and answer her, my voice loud enough for everyone to hear, "And now I will help him. But just me."

It seems like I should say more, or say something eloquent, but I am not well yet, barely back from the brink, my head pounding, and that is all the eloquence I am capable of.

I move slowly, straightening the Harris Z's right leg. It's the femur that is broken and the grating sound of the bone popping back into place along with the stench this close to the Z is hard to endure.

I take two of the sticks, placing one on each side of his broken femur and wrap it tight with rope. By the time I'm done, Wade and Meryl are back and I have more supplies to choose from.

I move slowly, carefully, like I'm treating an injured wild animal. I can feel Harris watching me, fighting his own instincts, but recognizing me for what I am, knowing that I am helping him.

Now that June is back, I don't pay attention to the crowd. I don't have the energy to spare. I just work, pulling the rope as tightly as I can, tying it securely, doing first aid on a zombie.

When I'm done, I stand up and step back. The Harris Z pushes up and slides his left leg underneath him and then his right until he is in an awkward kneeling position.

He lurches up, wobbles from side to side, and then takes a halting step forward and then another one. I hear some noisy sighs behind me as if half the folks had been holding their breath, expecting the Harris Z to attack me, expecting the three unrestrained Zs still in the pen to join him.

The Harris Z looks strange, more strange than the yellow-eyed, chewed-up zombie norm, the top of his legs practically mummied in rope, the two sticks on each femur making him whole again. Well, as whole as a piece of kind-of-dead rotting flesh can be.

He looks at me and I can feel the question. He wants to know if I will do for the others what I did for him. I nod and—most shocking of all—he nods back.

The gesture is fumbling and odd, but clearly recognizable. There are some gasps and I hear Dallas softly cursing and, as if on cue, the Al zombie shuffles out and falls to the ground and looks at me, his yellow zombie eyes once again reminding me of a hurt animal.

Is this what a cease fire in a war feels like? Because it feels tenuous as hell on top of being terrifying. But I do my part. I patch up each Z one by one until all four of them are awkwardly standing and staring back at the Talia Z.

They want something else from me and this time it's even more obvious. All this while Milo and Ralph have been holding on to the ropes restraining the Talia Z as I tended to the four others. She's been hissing and grasping and trying to move the whole time, acting like we are used to zombies acting.

I close and latch the gate, and the four Zs, the four former members of Phantom Company, shamble down the trail towards the river and don't look back.

I step back from the gate and Milo and Ralph let the Talia Z free, and she comes shambling across the pen reaching for me. I step back farther than I need to. I think I've got a healthy dose of Talia PTSD even though the worst she can do now is try to eat me.

And I'm sure she wants to eat me with every fiber of her kind-of-dead body.

When I turn back, everyone is staring at me.

Their looks worry me. They are wondering if I am human, if I am trustworthy, if I am worth the risk. Or, at least, I think that is what they are thinking.

My cheeks flush hot and I do my best to smile. "Thank you," I say. "I think that was important. I think that will make a difference."

Meryl nods and gives me a grim smile. "Yes, it was important," he says in his monotone. "Because we're not like her. We're not like them."

I blink and feel a wave of gratitude flow through me. Meryl was listening. He heard the lesson June taught me when she knocked Dallas out instead of killing her.

"We're not like them," a young woman says, and I know they were all listening.

"We're not like them," Lisa says, and the call goes up through the group.

"We're not like them. We're not like them. We're not like them."

CHAPTER TWENTY

THAT NIGHT, after the sun goes down and the flashlights and lanterns come out, we feast.

Everyone is in the dining hall. There's venison steaks, boiled baby potatoes, carrots, and even some salad. It's not like the old days, there's not enough food so you can stuff yourself full to bursting, but there is enough so that you can feel satisfied, like you actually got enough food, enough good food for once.

That's a rare thing these days.

A couple of joints get passed around and there is a noticeable lack of alcohol. My guess is that it's a lack of grains being grown because you know as soon as there are excess grains there will be alcohol.

After the meal is over, the tables are pushed to the side and a guitar, a small drum, and a fiddle come out. Meryl is playing the guitar and Lisa and a couple of others are singing. The music is folk, I think, or maybe bluegrass. I'm not real clear on the distinction. But the music is peppy and the lyrics speak of home and family and love.

People dance on the old wooden floor of the Phantom Ranch dining hall and it's a beautiful moment. I have a full belly, I'm not on the run from a psychotic, petty, wannabe warlord, I'm with the people I care about the most, and it's starting to seem like I may have found the place I was looking for.

I'm sitting on one of the tables, watching, but I still feel uneasy. It's not just the lingering pain from the fight or the whisper of the zombie group mind, it's something else but I can't quite put my finger on it.

"Penny," June says, hopping up on the table next to me.

"This is great," I say, leaning close so she can hear me and smell a soapy, clean June that I just want to keep breathing in. I nod towards the dancers and the band.

"But..." she prompts.

I shrug, and because of her prompt, it comes into focus. "We've been running so long now that it... it doesn't feel normal. I feel like I forgot something. Something really important."

She gives me a quirky smile. "Like in the old days when you're out but keep thinking you left the stove on and are going to come home to a burnt down house."

"Exactly," I say. "And you?"

She gives me a thin-lipped smile and nods. "I fear I'm not much of a homesteader. Churning butter is not my kind of thing."

Even though we are in a room full of people and noise, it feels like it's just the two of us, like this is the kind of simple, intimate moment I always longed for.

I see Dallas and Milo dancing and laughing. Dallas is definitely favoring her right foot, still not completely recovered, but she looks so happy. Milo lifts her and twirls her around. She giggles with such bright enthusiasm, I can't help but smile.

"In any case," June says. "A couple more days and you'll be well enough. We can go try to find Wade's family."

I nod.

"Do you think they'll be okay down here?" she asks, nodding at the revelers.

I nod. "There's still enough human in them to understand the concept of territory, and I've claimed this. I think patching up the

Harris zombie and the others and letting them go underscored that. As long as we are not gone too long, it should be okay."

"But we shouldn't count on the Zs staying put," she says.

"Better defenses are needed," I say. "From the Zs and the living."

"You know," she says, leaning closer. "I learned a lot treating you this time. When we're out there, if we can find the right drugs, you might be able to totally kick the infection."

She looks at me with a neutral expression, but the statement is more than a little loaded. She's trying to find out how attached I am to being part of the zombie group mind.

I nod. "It's complicated, June."

One eyebrow raises and she asks, "Zs are people too?"

I shake my head. "Not quite. I mean, I'd rather not kill them, but I certainly will. It's clear the Zs aren't quite what we thought they were, but we are still their food supply. I keep thinking that there's more to learn. Maybe when we're back here and really ready for a siege, that might make sense. But not yet. I..."

I lose my train of thought and watch the dancers, watch the way Milo looks at Dallas, and I am happy for her. Watching her smile and laugh, exhibiting the simplest human expressions of joy, something that has been so rare in my recent life, I realize how precious it is.

"What is it, Woody?" June asks, leaning into me, our elbows bumping together.

The thought comes back to me and it's not one I want to share, but this is June. "I'm learning from them," I say slowly, quietly. "But they are learning from me."

June swallows, her eyes darting away. "Like the tactics they used to take out Talia's people," she says.

I nod. I told her about the dreams that weren't dreams.

She grabs my arm and leans her head against me. "There's no easy choices now," she says. "No clear path. No knowing what it means. We are alive now because they learned from you."

"But should they learn any more from me?" I ask.

She takes my face in her hands and I am bathed in the ocean-blue of her eyes. "We don't have the drugs to do more than keep you stable," she says. "So let it go. Let's enjoy this moment."

She gets up and grabs my hand and pulls me onto the dance floor. I groan, not because I don't know how to dance or don't like to dance, but because I am sore all over and am still recovering from the beating Talia gave me.

But this is June, my June, and I can't resist.

She leads me into something of a two-step and soon my body loosens up and we're dancing and laughing with everyone else.

DANCING IS good for the soul. I don't know why, but it is. Maybe it's the physical intimacy of it. Maybe it's an icebreaker that lets you get to know others under clearly defined social rules. Maybe it's that it's inherently joyful.

Maybe this should be added to my list of goals for each post-apocalypse day after survive, laugh, and spend time with June. Number 4, dance a little. If you can stand, you can dance. Hell, if you can sit up, you can dance. I forgot how great it is to move just for the sake of moving—in other words, not running from Zs or psychotic, petty, wannabe warlords, or just trying to survive.

And Phantom Ranch really needs the celebration because the dancing goes on and on. Some line dancing. Some two-step. Some freestyle, move your body any way you want, dancing.

At one point Dallas and I are dancing, the free-style variety, and what used to be her frown lines are smile lines tonight.

"Going good with Milo?" I ask.

She nods, her smile getting wider. "I might not die a spinster after all."

It's a small thing but I feel a wash of emotion and tears sting at my eyes. While Dallas dramatically moaned about being a spinster, it was a real possibility.

"This makes me happy," I say.

"But we still have a deal, right?" she asks. She wiggles her eyebrows ridiculously, along with her hips, to make sure I know we are talking about having a child.

"If June's on board," I say. "I am."

She gives me a leering look and comes closer and says, "If June's on board you'll be getting on board." She laughs and I smell alcohol on her breath. I'm not sure where she got it, but this being Dallas it's not that much of a surprise.

I don't know what the look on my face is, but I can tell you that I am still feeling confused by it all and it must have shown. "Don't worry, Woody," she says. "I'll be gentle."

The music stops and the dancers clear away. It looks like the band is taking a break and I'm just standing there like a dummy looking at Dallas.

She comes up and whispers, "You know I'm on team Woody and June, all the way. And I'm your best friend. Here's proof." She slips something into my front pocket. "She's been wondering since you promised to ask her a question when waiting for Talia at the bridge. Now would be a very good time."

There's no mistaking what she slipped into my pocket. It's a ring box and my heart starts hammering in my chest as Dallas gives a loud whoop and goes over to Milo, leaving me standing in the middle of the dance floor alone.

People are staring at me. Honestly, since all the madness with Talia and my blind fighting and zombie first-aid routines, I get a lot of looks. Some full of curiosity, some full of awe, some fearful as people take pains to avoid me.

And I get it. Can I be trusted? Am I safe? It's, honestly, better than I expected. They haven't grabbed torches and pitchforks and formed a mob to chase me out of town, but it's still not comfortable.

But now, it's something different. Like they know what Dallas just gave me, like they want me to do what I'm terrified to do.

"Something on your mind there, Woody?" Lisa calls out, the amusement in her voice clear.

I've babbled on about the preciousness of life and how I will cherish these socially awkward situations because they mean I have the gift of life, that I am safe enough to have them. And that is certainly true, but it doesn't change the feeling of it. I want to puke, the room suddenly feels very hot, and I feel sweat pricking on the back of my neck.

I look around and find June. She's looking down, her hands shoved in the pocket of her jeans. She slowly raises her head, a shy look on her face. She's nervous too. The woman that was eager to take on Talia is nervous about the question she must know I want to ask, and this makes me feel like I'm not alone.

And I'm not. That's the point. It's not Woody versus the Apocalypse anymore. It's Woody and June and Dallas and Phantom Ranch versus the Apocalypse.

I can feel the energy in the room shift as the rest of them figure out what's happening, and all the other conversations stop.

"I love you, June Medina," I say.

She looks down and says, "I love you, Woody Beckman."

And there it is. The true miracle that has occurred. We survived the Zs, we survived the elements, we survived Talia, and there is friendship, partnership, and love left over.

I walk over and take her hand and draw her into the center of the circle. All eyes are on us, but it feels like we are alone.

"It's the weirdest thing," I say, trying to find the right words. "The happiest days of my life happened after the apocalypse. They've all been since I met you."

She looks up and her beautiful blue eyes almost take my breath away. She gives me a shy smile and nods for me to continue.

"These haven't been easy days or safe days or even sane days, but they've been happy days. You are the strongest, most courageous woman I've ever known, and I am honored to be your friend and your partner."

She swallows hard and her eyes glisten with pending tears.

"I don't know what the future holds or how many days I have left in this insane world, but I want to spend each of them with you."

She nods, this time it seems like she's nodding in agreement. She doesn't say anything, and that's fine with me. This is proving to be harder than I had even feared.

I slowly get down on one knee and suppress a groan, my body still sore and recovering.

I pull the ring box out of my jeans, hold it up to June, pop it open, and say, "June Medina, will you do me the honor of marrying me?"

There's silence in the room, and except for my lingering extra senses from the Z-mind, it's almost the silence of the apocalypse. June stares at the ring and then her wide eyes find mine.

Was I wrong in that she knew what I was going to ask? Was Dallas off too? Was this the stupidest thing I've ever done, and I am destined to die alone? Were my words not sufficient to communicate what is in my heart?

In those few moments, that seemed like hours, those kinds of thoughts rage through my head and I feel my cheeks flush red and realize that despite the joy of survival, despite the fungal infection my body is still fighting, that I am still quite human. This fear of social rejection an undeniable sign of my humanity.

That realization takes the edge off, but still my heart gallops along as June looks at the ring and then looks back at me.

So then I have to wonder if the ring is terrible. I didn't even have a chance to look at it. Did Dallas set me up here?

But then June takes the ring out of the box and I can see why her eyes were so wide. It's a hell of a diamond on a gold band, maybe three carats, and even though such things don't have much value anymore, it is a thing of sublime beauty glittering in the makeshift light of flashlights and lanterns.

She slips the ring on her left hand and by some miracle it fits. Well, that miracle being Dallas who really is my best friend.

June swallows hard and says, "My life was all darkness before I met you, Woody. I was alone and determined to stay that way. But from the moment we met, despite the dire circumstances, you tried to make me laugh. Despite all the close calls and madness, you stood by me and tried to find the joy in each day. So yes, Woody Beckman. I will marry you. Today. Tomorrow. Every day."

And then there is cheering and then June is in my arms and then all of Phantom Ranch is around us in one big hug.

The party goes on for a very long time.

EPILOGUE

THE FUTURE IS UNCERTAIN, but it has always been this way, even before the zombies came.

The past is dark and troubling, even before the apocalypse it was for many, and it is for all now.

The apocalypse has taught me to take every moment, every joy, every experience in to the best of my ability. To find the gift in the good, the bad, and the fetid that comes my way.

As we crest the rim on the Bright Angel Trail and we smell the fetid bouquet of the Zs that are assembled here, I say, "I love the smell of zombies in the morning."

June groans and Dallas says, "Shut up, Woody." But her voice isn't serious.

It's not just the three of us this time. Milo is with us, which is not surprising—he's rarely far away from Dallas these days. Wade is here, it's his family we are going to try to find. And Lisa is part of the group too.

Everyone is dressed in the uniform of the apocalypse. Hiking boots, the best you can find that fit you, jeans, a T-shirt, preferably a technical shirt that can wick your sweat away, and an overstuffed backpack bristling with food, survival gear, and weapons.

I smile and adjust my Grand Canyon baseball hat. I don't expect all of my very bad jokes to land. It's the effort that counts.

"Are they going to let us through?" June asks, referring to those zombies I just so lamely joked about.

As I healed, June decreased my steroid dose so it's fairly small now. As that has happened, my connection to the zombie group mind has gotten stronger again, but now I am more used to it so it's not quite as troubling.

We think the extra zombie scratches I got during the fight with Talia is what triggered the latest crisis, but my body and the fungus seemed to have found a new point of balance.

"Yes," I say. We are walking past the historic log cabins and coming out in front of the Bright Angel Lodge with its lovely stonework and big wooden beams.

Besides the smell, I can hear the collective snarl of them floating in on the light breeze.

"Will they stay here?" Lisa asks. She's got a bandana covering her short black hair and her dark skin is glistening with sweat.

As we walk down into the parking lot in front of the lodge, we can see some of them. Down a hill from us, across a road and then a set of train tracks is a building several stories tall made out of Kaibab limestone. Next to it is a tangle of electrical transformers. There are about twenty of them milling about there.

"I believe so," I say. "They know my mind and they know I mean to come back. That we might be chased back. That whoever chases us is fair game for them."

Dallas snorts. "So we're bait for them?"

I nod. "Something like that."

Dallas still has her bite, but she has softened. She's busy signing to Milo as we talk. I don't know sign language, and Dallas doesn't know a lot either, but she's learning and knows some common words and all the letters of the alphabet. She ends up spelling out a lot of things to him. It's sweet, but I would never tell her that.

104 ROBERT J. MCCARTER

I'm thinking we all should learn it. Being able to communicate silently could come in handy these days.

I close my eyes and tap into the zombie group mind. The Zs are spread out all over the village and there are enough of them spaced out here and there that I can feel them all the way to Desert View. They, of course, know we are here and I don't feel any particular interest in us on their part.

I send them the images of the six of us getting into two vehicles and driving away and then coming back a few days later. Again, nothing particular comes back from the group mind. This is old news —they've known this as long as I have.

"Where are the vehicles?" I ask Lisa.

She points to the south and says, "They're stashed in the mule barn. They are beat to hell, so as not to stand out, but they'll get us there."

"You ready for this?" I ask Wade. "You ready to go find Alison, Jessica, and your wife?"

With his glasses, the grey invading his curly black hair, and middle-age bulge, he doesn't look like he's up for the dangers ahead. I've called him a geek, but he's also a father and a husband and he's already proven himself willing to take chances on their behalf.

He looks nervous and nods. "There's another one of your wannabe warlords in charge by now," he says.

"But we've got Woody and his undead army," Dallas says.

They are most definitely not my undead army, but I'm done trying to correct Dallas on that. She's just probably teasing anyway.

"How do you think the Flagstaff Zs will react to you?" June asks.

I shrug, which isn't very effective with a heavy backpack on, and it just makes those latest zombie scratches hurt more. "Maybe they'll be curious like the pods were at first. Maybe they'll consider me an anomaly and attack. Who knows?"

Wade's eyes get wide, June just gives me a grim nod, and Dallas whoops, points both her middle fingers to the south and says, "Here we come, Flagstaff! One way or another you won't forget us anytime soon!"

There's some nervous chuckles and the group heads out towards some metal stairs that lead down to the tracks where the tourist train used to stop, but I just stay there and so does June.

I take my hat off, wipe the sweat from my forehead, and put it back on. It's cooler up here, but we climbed out fast and I'm still hot. My fingers brush the still healing wound where Talia tried to blow my head off, but it feels different now that Talia is a Z stuck in a pen down at Phantom Ranch.

"You like your new hat," June says.

I smile and nod. It's not the red Diamondbacks hat I clung to so fiercely when June and I met, the one that linked me to my past. This one is a dark blue and is a fairly touristy Grand Canyon hat. "This is our home now. Our new life." I nod towards the four others who are heading down the stairs now. "They are our new family. It fits."

I'm smiling as I'm watching the four of them. Dallas and Lisa are chattering away and signing at the same time. Milo has this slow lumbering gate that easily matches pace with the quicker walk of the shorter women.

Dallas has a slight limp, and maybe she always will, but she seems really good. I can't hear what they're saying but Dallas hops up, grabs the baseball cap Milo is wearing, and runs down the metal stairs that lead to the train tracks, a delighted yell ringing out as Milo gives chase.

All of this in the presence of Zs. I don't know why, but witnessing this little scene lets it really sink in that things are different.

When I glance back at June, she is staring at me with a thoughtful smile on her face. "So it's not just Woody and June versus the Apocalypse anymore?" she asks.

"Oh no," I say, smiling and shaking my head. "It's definitely Woody and June versus the Apocalypse. Today. Tomorrow. Every day."

She smiles a real smile and it's a dazzling thing that makes me smile even more. "Woody and June versus the Apocalypse," she says. "*Siempre!*"

She takes my hand, and feeling her engagement ring there, with its big fat diamond, just strengthens the feeling. As we walk after our growing family and towards our future, I don't know what's next or how long we'll have, but I do know that we will give it everything we've got, that we'll hold tight to our humanity, that we'll laugh every chance we get, and dance a little bit every now and then.

MORE ADVENTURE?

WANT another story in the world of Woody and June? When you subscribe to my newsletter you'll get a free 750+ page ebook, *Bits, Bites, and Rarities: The Worlds of Robert J. McCarter*, that introduces you to my many series, and has four stories you can't read anywhere else including "Park's Law of the Apocalypse," a novelette that takes place in the world of Woody and June. Find out more at RobertJMcCarter.com/newsletter.

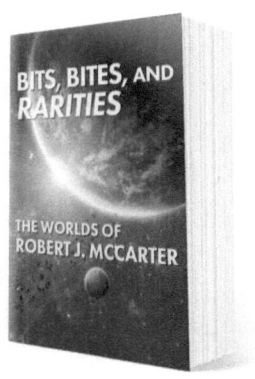

Until there is more Woody and June to read, remember that your life is an adventure and no matter what current "apocalypse" is befalling you, love hard, be kind, and take it all in stride.

IF YOU ENJOYED THIS BOOK, you might be interested in my superhero / love story series: *Neutrinoman & Lightningirl: A Love*

Story. In this series I take a similar spin on the superhero genre as I did here with zombies. Real characters in extraordinary situations that are full of adventure, fun, and romance. Season 1 and 2 are out. All the details are below:

SUPERHEROES... FALLING IN LOVE... SAVING THE WORLD

Follow Nik Nichols (aka Neutrinoman) and Licia Lopez (aka Lightningirl) on this wild adventure past "happily ever after" into the heart of love while they try to protect the Earth from aliens bent on our destruction.

Join my newsletter and get the first episode ebook, *Meteor Attack!*, for free!

Each episode is available separately, but buy a season at a time for the best value.

Season 1: Episodes 1 - 3

- Meteor Attack!: Falling in love and saving the world...
- Toxic Asset: Friend or Enemy?
- Protocol X: An Alien Encounter

Season 2: Episodes 4 - 6

- Off Book: An impossible mission...
- Hard Times: Everything will change...
- Elemental Factors: A team arises

ABOUT THE AUTHOR

Robert J. McCarter is the author of more than ten novels and over a hundred short stories. He is a regular contributor to *Pulphouse Fiction Magazine* and his short fiction has also appeared in *The Saturday Evening Post, Andromeda Spaceways Inflight Magazine, Everyday Fiction*, and numerous anthologies.

Robert writes in a variety of genres from contemporary fantasy to science fiction and just about everything in between. His diverse background–including a career in software engineering, growing up on a ranch riding horses, and acting–colors the stories he tells.

He lives in the mountains of Arizona with his amazing wife and his ridiculously adorable dogs.

Find out more at:
RobertJMcCarter.com

BOOKS BY ROBERT J. MCCARTER

WOODY AND JUNE VERSUS THE APOCALYPSE

For a great deal, pick up *Woody and June Versus the Apocalypse* a volume at at time!

Woody and June Versus the Apocalypse: Volume 1 (Episodes 1 - 7)

- Woody and June versus the Wannabe Warlord
- Woody and June versus the Fungus-Head Zombies
- Woody and June versus the Grand Canyon
- Woody and June versus the Ex
- Woody and June versus the Third Wheel
- Woody and June versus Phantom Company
- Woody and June versus the Daring Rescue

Woody and June Versus the Apocalypse: Volume 2 (Episodes 8 - 12)

- Woody and June versus the Chase
- Woody and June versus Two Guns
- Woody and June versus Winslow
- Woody and June versus the Infection
- Woody and June versus the Siege

Woody and June Versus the Apocalypse: Volume 3 (Episodes 13 - 17)

- Woody and June versus the Pod

- Woody and June versus the Impossible Choice
- Woody and June versus the Reunion
- Woody and June versus the Standoff
- Woody and June versus the End

Find out more at WoodyAndJune.com

NEUTRINOMAN & LIGHTNINGIRL: A LOVE STORY

For a great deal, pick up *Neutrinoman & Lightningirl: A Love Story* a season at at time!

Season 1 (Omnibus edition of Episodes 1 - 3)

- Meteor Attack!
- Toxic Asset
- Protocol X

Season 2 (Omnibus edition of Episodes 4-6)

- Off Book
- Hard Times
- Elemental Factors

Find out the latest at Neutrinoman.com

For a complete list of books, go to RobertJMcCarter.com/books

www.ingramcontent.com/pod-product-compliance
Lightning Source LLC
Chambersburg PA
CBHW020415130626
46549CB00006B/2569